Dirty Bertie

MAYHEM and MISCHIEF

DAVID ROBERTS WRITTEN BY ALAN MACDONALD

Stripes

Collect all the
Dirty Bertie books!

Contents

STRIPES PUBLISHING
An imprint of Little Tiger Press
1 The Coda Centre, 189 Munster Road,
London SW6 6AW

A paperback original
First published in Great Britain in 2012

ISBN: 978-1-84715-253-4

Characters created by David Roberts
Text copyright © Alan MacDonald
Burp! 2007 • *Yuck!* 2008 • *Bogeys!* 2009
Illustrations copyright © David Roberts
Burp! 2007 • *Yuck!* 2008 • *Bogeys!* 2009

Printed and bound in the UK.

10 9 8 7 6 5 4 3 2 1

For Henry, who seems to have picked
up some of Bertie's dirty habits
(apologies to the hamster) ~ D R

Contents

CHAPTER 1

Bertie was the only one in his class who
actually liked school dinners. Lumpy
mash with gloopy gravy. Wormy spaghetti
with meatballs. Cold custard with slimy
skin on top. Bertie loved them all.

"Ugh! I don't know how you can eat
it!" said Darren at lunch on Friday. Bertie
slurped his rice pudding and gave an

extremely satisfied burp.

"Aren't you going to finish yours?"

"No," said Darren. "It looks like frogspawn."

"Pass it over," said Bertie.

Just then Miss Skinner, the Head, swept into the dining hall with a woman in a white coat. Miss Skinner rapped on a table to get their attention. "I want you all to meet Miss Beansprout, who is our new Head Dinner Lady," she said. "Miss Beansprout has lots of splendid ideas to improve our school meals."

Dirty Bertie

Miss Beansprout gazed at them fondly. "Children," she said, "it's my job to make sure you all have a healthy, wholesome diet. Who can tell me something that is healthy and delicious?"

Pamela raised her hand. "An orange," she said.

"Very good," beamed Miss Beansprout.

"An avocado," said Know-All Nick, showing off.

"Excellent," said Miss Beansprout.

"Nuts," said Bertie.

"Wonderful. Nuts are very good for you," nodded Miss Beansprout.

"Great," said Bertie. "Will we be having doughnuts tomorrow?"

"Stop talking and get on with your dinner," snapped Miss Beansprout.

On Monday Mrs Mould wasn't serving dinners behind the hatch as usual. In her place was Miss Beansprout. She had written a menu on the board.

Today's Menu
Cabbage and chickpea Soup
Broccoli Bake with Beetroot Salad
Carrot cake Surprise
Low-Fat Yoghurt
apple or banana (for a treat)

Bertie and his friends stared in horror. Surely this was some kind of joke? *Broccoli? Cabbage?* Was she trying to KILL them?

"What's this?" asked Bertie.

"Lots of lovely fruit and vegetables," said Miss Beansprout. "Just what growing children need."

"But where are the chips?" asked Bertie.

"No greasy chips," said Miss Beansprout.

"Where is the custard?"

"No horrible custard."

"Where's the jam roly-poly pudding?"

"No stodgy puddings full of nasty sugar," said Miss Beansprout. "From now on we're all going to be eating delicious greens and nourishing salads."

"I love salad," said Know-All Nick. "A big helping for me!"

13

Bertie gave him a withering look.

"Cabbage Soup or Broccoli Bake?"
Miss Beansprout asked him.

"Can't I just have pudding?" asked
Bertie.

"Broccoli Bake it is," said Miss
Beansprout. She ladled a gloopy green
mess on to Bertie's plate. SPLAT!

Next to it went the salad, swimming in beetroot juice.

"Yoghurt or Carrot Cake Surprise?" asked Miss Beansprout.

"What's the surprise?" asked Bertie, hopefully.

"The carrots are organic. That means they're bursting with vitamins!" beamed Miss Beansprout.

Bertie carried his tray over to a table to sit down. "I can't eat this," he grumbled, staring at his plate.

"You haven't tasted it yet," said Know-All Nick.

"Quite right, Nicholas," said Miss Skinner, who was on dinner duty. "Perhaps some *fussy* children could learn from your example. Eat up, Bertie, it looks delicious!"

Dirty Bertie

Bertie raised a forkful of green gloop to his lips. Darren leaned over to whisper in his ear.

"Boiled bogeys with squashed slug salad."

Bertie set down his fork. Suddenly he didn't feel at all hungry.

CHAPTER 2

Miss Beansprout's dinners got worse. On Tuesday they had Celery and Nut Crumble. On Wednesday it was Liver Casserole and Sprouts followed by Stewed Prunes. Bertie couldn't take any more. At break time he called an emergency meeting in the playground.

"If I eat one more vegetable I'm going

to be sick," he groaned.

"So am I," said Eugene.

"I couldn't stop burping yesterday," said Darren. "Great big smelly burps!"

"I know, I was sitting next to you," moaned Donna.

"Well it's no good just grumbling, we've got to do something," said Bertie.

"We could kidnap Miss Beansprout and lock her in a dungeon," suggested Darren.

"Good idea," said Donna. "Except we haven't got a dungeon."

"Well I'm not putting up with it any longer," said Bertie. "They can't make us eat it."

"Can't they?" asked Eugene.

"No," said Bertie. "Not if we all refuse. Not if we all say we're going on strike."

Dirty Bertie

Eugene looked anxious. "Won't we get into trouble?"

"Listen," said Bertie. "We're not eating anything until they give us back our old dinners. Right?"

"Right," agreed the others. Even lumpy mash and gloopy gravy would be better than the sickly slop Miss Beansprout gave them.

At lunchtime Bertie joined the dinner queue.

"What would you like? Liver Casserole and Sprouts?" asked Miss Beansprout.

"No, thank you," said Bertie.

"A big slice of Spinach Pie?"

"No thanks," said Bertie. "I don't want anything."

"Nothing? Don't be silly. You have to eat," said Miss Beansprout.

Bertie shook his head firmly. "I'd rather go without."

"So would I," said Darren.

"And me," said Donna. She nudged Eugene.

"Oh, me too … please," said Eugene.

Dirty Bertie

Miss Beansprout sent for Miss Skinner. "These children are refusing to eat their dinner," she said.

"Which children?" said Miss Skinner. The others all looked at Bertie.

"We're on strike," Bertie informed her. "Till you bring back the old dinners."

Miss Skinner smiled a thin smile. "I see. You don't want any dinner? Well that's fine with me."

"Pardon?" said Bertie.

"It's fine. Go without," said Miss Skinner. "Off you go!"

Dirty Bertie

Bertie and his friends trooped away with empty plates. They sat down at a table and watched the other children chewing and slurping their food.

"I'm hungry," moaned Darren.

"So am I," groaned Eugene.

"I'm starving! I could even eat a carrot," said Donna.

Eugene gazed over at Know-All Nick's plate. "Couldn't we just have pudding?"

"NO!" said Bertie. "We're on strike, remember? We're not eating until they give us back our old dinners."

"But I haven't had anything since breakfast," grumbled Darren. "If I don't eat soon I'll starve to death!"

"Huh!" said Bertie. "Well it would just serve them right if we did. Maybe it'd teach them a lesson."

Dirty Bertie

CHAPTER 3

SLAM! Bertie arrived home from school. His mum was in the kitchen talking on the phone.

"Yes," she said. "Don't worry, I'll speak to him. He's just come in now."

Bertie had the feeling it was time to make a swift exit. He ran upstairs.

"BERTIE!" yelled his mum. "Down here

now. I want a word with you."

Bertie shuffled into the kitchen.

"What's all this about not eating your school dinners?" demanded Mum.

"Oh," said Bertie. "That."

"Yes, that. I just had Miss Skinner on the phone and she sounds very cross."

"It's not my fault," said Bertie. "The dinners are horrible! They're full of vegetables."

"Vegetables are good for you."

"But Mum, they're making us eat broccoli. And beetroot! And carrots!"

"Good," said Mum. "It sounds very healthy."

"How can it be healthy when I feel ill just looking at it?" asked Bertie.

"Don't make such a fuss, Bertie. It's only a few carrots!"

Dirty Bertie

"But Mum…"

"No buts," said Mum. "Tomorrow you eat all your dinner."

Bertie sighed. "OK."

"Promise me," said Mum.

"I promise," said Bertie.

As he went upstairs he smiled to himself. He'd promised to eat his dinner – but he hadn't said what would be in it, had he?

Dirty Bertie

PEEP! Miss Skinner blew her whistle for the start of school. Bertie hurriedly stuffed something down his jumper and fell into line.

"What if she catches you?" hissed Darren.

"She won't," replied Bertie.

"No talking at the back!" yelled Miss Skinner. "In you go."

The line of children began to file past the Head, who watched them with narrowed eyes. Bertie kept his head down. Another few metres and he was home and dry. An arm shot out and barred his way. Uh oh.

"Bertie," said Miss Skinner.

"Yes, Miss?"

Dirty Bertie

"What's that lump under your jumper?"

"Lump, Miss? Nothing, Miss."

"Really?" Miss Skinner's finger prodded his jumper. It crackled and rustled.

"Hands up," ordered the Head Teacher.

"What?" said Bertie.

"You heard me, hands in the air."

Bertie raised both his hands. A bag of crisps fell out of his jumper. Then two more.

"Pockets," said Miss Skinner.

Bertie turned out his pockets. Some sweets and chocolate bars scattered at Miss Skinner's feet.

"You know the rules, Bertie," she said. "No crisps or sweets in school." The chocolate disappeared into her pocket.

Dirty Bertie

Later that day, Bertie passed the staff room on his way to lunch. He heard raised voices inside. "Thank goodness we don't have to survive on school dinners," said Miss Boot.

"Yes, they really are unpleasant," replied Miss Skinner. "Have another piece."

Bertie opened the door a crack and peeped in.

Dirty Bertie

He could see his teachers eating something. It was a bar of chocolate. *His* bar of chocolate. Bertie gasped. Well this time they'd gone too far. Nobody stole Bertie's chocolate and got away with it.

In the dining room Bertie stared. All his friends were eating their dinner.

"I thought we were on strike," Bertie scowled.

"Sorry, Bertie. I've got to eat. My mum made me promise," replied Eugene.

"Mine too," said Darren.

"Never mind, at least we tried," sighed Donna.

Bertie didn't answer. He wasn't beaten yet. If only he could think of some way to get revenge. He stared at the sloppy cauliflower cheese on Eugene's plate…

"It looks disgusting," he said.

"Yeah," agreed Darren. "Like flies in custard."

"Worms in ice cream," said Donna.

"Maggot jelly," said Eugene.

Bertie's mouth fell open. Why hadn't he thought of it before? Miss Beansprout was always boasting that her meals were made with fresh ingredients… Well maybe he would add a few fresh ingredients of his own!

CHAPTER 4

Next day Bertie waited impatiently for
break time.

BRIIING! The bell sounded and the
class thundered out into the playground.
Bertie doubled back and slipped across
the dining hall to the kitchen. He pushed
open the door to check the coast was
clear. Miss Beansprout was humming to

herself at the sink in the back room. He would have to move fast. Bertie tiptoed over to the fridge and opened the door.

There on the top shelf was his target – a large bowl full of green salad. Bertie pulled out the tin he'd borrowed from his dad's fishing bag and took off the lid. Inside was a sea of fat wriggling grubs.

"Dinner time, boys!" he whispered.

Half an hour later, Miss Skinner sat down to eat her lunch. She raised a forkful of green salad to her mouth and began to chew. Strange, she thought, today it tasted rather odd – sort of salty and squishy. She gazed down at her plate.

Something in the salad moved. It raised
its head and wiggled around.

"ARGHHHHH!" screamed Miss
Skinner. "MAGGOTS!"

Her plate smashed on the floor. She clutched at her throat. Maggots! And she had just swallowed a whole mouthful! She grabbed a jug of water and glugged it down.

"Miss Beansprout!" she screeched. The Head Dinner Lady came running.

Everywhere she looked children were yelling, screaming and spitting their food on the floor. What on earth was going on?

"Look!" thundered Miss Skinner pointing at her plate. "Look!"

"I … I don't understand," stammered Miss Beansprout. "The salad was fresh this morning."

"Fresh?" thundered Miss Skinner. "It's crawling with maggots! Are you trying to poison me?"

Dirty Bertie

"I'm sorry, Miss Skinner. It won't happen again."

"You're right, Miss Beansprout," fumed the Head. "It certainly won't."

The following Monday Bertie was back in the lunch queue once again. The board with today's healthy menu had vanished. There was no sign of Miss Beansprout. Mrs Mould was back behind the hatch in her grubby apron. Bertie couldn't wait. *No more yucky beetroot or boring broccoli,* he thought, *mash and gravy here I come!*

Mrs Mould slopped a pile of spaghetti on to his plate. Bertie stared. It was sticky, wriggling and wiggling.

Just like…

He clapped a hand over his mouth
and fled from the dining room.

"What's wrong with him?" asked
Eugene.

"Dunno," shrugged Darren. "I thought
he liked wormy spaghetti."

CHAPTER 1

Bertie was busy working on an
experiment in his bedroom. For weeks
now he had been collecting the
ingredients to make a stink bomb.

Bertie's Super-smelly STINKBOMB - Mark ①

1 lump of pongy cheese   1 sweaty football sock
4 rotten eggs   3 mouldy cabbage leaves
1 tin of dog food   ① Dog hairs - a goodhandful

Dirty Bertie

Slip! Slop! Bertie gave the ingredients
a good stir with a pencil and sniffed the
murky brown goo. *Not bad*, he thought.

It just needed a few more days to get
really good and pongy. Bertie couldn't
wait to try out his stink bomb at school.
Maybe he could smuggle it into Miss
Boot's desk? Or, better still, splat Know-
All Nick on the way home from
school. Whiffer padded over and
poked his nose into the
plastic pot.

"Uh uh. No,
Whiffer," said
Bertie. "It's not
for eating."

Someone was coming. Bertie quickly
slammed the lid on the pot and hid it in
his bedside cupboard.

Dirty Bertie

Mum poked her head around the door. "Bertie, what are you doing?" she asked suspiciously.

"Nothing," said Bertie. "Just playing."

Mum sniffed the air. "What's that funny smell?"

"Smell? I can't smell anything."

"It's disgusting," said Mum. "It smells like a family of skunks!"

"Does it?" Bertie looked pleased. The stink bomb must be a real humdinger if you could smell it from inside a cupboard. Mum was sniffing round the room trying to detect where the nasty smell was coming from. Bertie knew he'd have to act quickly before she investigated the bedside cupboard.

"PHEW, WHIFFER! Was that you?" he said, holding his nose.

Whiffer wagged his tail.

"That dog," sighed Mum. She turned back to Bertie. "I thought I asked you to tidy your room."

"It *is* tidy," replied Bertie.

Mum gave him a withering look. "Bertie! There's rubbish everywhere!"

Bertie inspected his room. Everything was where it normally was. On the floor.

"I like it like this," he explained.

"Well, I don't and I need you to tidy it up," said Mum. "Suzy's having a friend for a sleepover tonight."

"Who?" asked Bertie.

Suzy appeared in the doorway. "Bella," she said.

Bertie groaned. Not Bossy Bella. Of all Suzy's friends she was the worst. She would be trying to boss him around all night.

"And they'll be sleeping in here," said Mum.

Bertie's mouth fell open. He felt sick, he felt dizzy. "HERE? In MY ROOM?" he said.

"Yes," said Mum. "Your room's much bigger than Suzy's. We can put up the Z bed."

"But ... but where am I going to sleep?"

"In Suzy's room."

Dirty Bertie

"NO!" yelled Bertie.

"NO!" screamed Suzy.

"It's only for one night," said Mum.

"I can't sleep in here. I'll catch fleas!" grumbled Suzy.

"Nonsense. Bertie's going to tidy up."

"Tidy up? It needs disinfecting!" said Suzy. "And what's that horrible smell?"

Mum pointed at Whiffer. "He needs to go back to the vet's."

CHAPTER 2

DING DONG! Bertie could hear voices downstairs. Bossy Bella had arrived.

"Hello, Bella!" said Mum brightly.

"Hello," replied Bella.

"Have a super time, pumpkin!" said Bella's mum, kissing her on the cheek. "I'll pick you up in the morning."

Mum shut the door.

"Well then, why don't you show Bella where she's sleeping, Suzy?"

Bella handed Suzy her suitcase and clumped upstairs after her.

They found Bertie on his bed reading a comic.

"Get out," said Suzy.

"You get out," said Bertie. "This is my room."

"Not tonight. Mum says we've got to sleep in here, remember?"

Bella scowled. She hated little brothers. If she had a little brother she would give him to a charity shop.

"I'm not sleeping in his bed," she pointed. "It smells."

"You're the one that smells," replied Bertie.

"You do."

"No, you do."

"No, you do."

"Ignore him," said Suzy. "Let's play princesses. You can be Princess Bella."

"Princess Smella, you mean," sniggered Bertie.

Bella yanked Bertie off the bed. She twisted his arm.

"OW!" cried Bertie. He gave her a shove. Bella stumbled and fell on to the Z bed. Twang! It collapsed.

"Waaaahhhh!" she howled.

Mum came running upstairs. "What's going on?" she demanded.

"Bertie hit me," whined Bella.

"Bertie!" said Mum, crossly.

"I didn't!" said Bertie. "She practically broke my arm!"

"It was him that started it," said Suzy. "He's spoiling our game."

"Bertie, go to your room!" ordered Mum.

"This is my room," said Bertie.

"I mean go to Suzy's room and stay there till supper."

Bertie stormed out. It wasn't fair. He'd get those sneaky girls for this.

Dirty Bertie

"Supper time!" called Mum.

Bertie bounded downstairs. He was
starving. He'd been in Suzy's room for
hours and there was nothing to play with.
Not even a pirate cutlass or water pistol.
In the kitchen he could smell pizza and
chips.

"Yum," said Bertie, helping himself to a
large slice of pizza.

"Manners, Bertie!" said Mum.

"Yes, Bertie," said Suzy. "We always
serve guests first."

Bertie reluctantly put the pizza back
and pushed the plate under Bella's nose.
Bella pulled a face. "I don't like pizza."

"Oh dear, never mind, have some
salad," said Mum.

Dirty Bertie

"I don't like salad," grumbled Bella.

"Then just eat the chips," sighed Mum, piling some on Bella's plate.

"I don't like these chips. They're not like my mum's," complained Bella.

"Great, all the more for me!" said Bertie, reaching over to grab Bella's plate.

"Bertie!" snapped Dad.

Bella grabbed her plate and held on. Bertie pulled. Bella pulled back. The chips

catapulted into the air and landed on
the floor.

Bertie bent down. He picked up a
chip, wiped it on his shirt and ate it.

"BERTIE!" yelled Mum.

"What did I do now?" asked Bertie
with his mouth full.

"Get down from the table and go to
your room!" ordered Mum.

Bella looked at Suzy. They both smiled.

CHAPTER 3

After supper the girls sat down to watch
TV. Bertie burst in and threw himself
into an armchair. "Where's the remote?
Alien Arthur is on!" he said.

"We're watching the other side," said
Suzy. "It's *Make Me a Pop Princess*."

"What?" gasped Bertie. "But I always
watch *Alien Arthur* on Saturdays."

Dirty Bertie

"Let's take a vote," said Suzy. "Who wants Bertie's programme?"

Bertie put up his hand.

"Who wants to watch *Pop Princess?*" Suzy and Bella both raised their hands.

"Two votes to one, you lose," sneered Bella.

Bertie slumped in his chair, miserably. This was turning out to be the worst Saturday ever. And it was all the fault of Suzy and her bossy friend. He couldn't even go up to his room to work on his stink bomb because Mum said he had to keep out. Well, he wasn't going to be beaten that easily. There was no way he was sleeping in Suzy's bedroom tonight. Her walls were covered in posters of ponies and drippy pop stars. It was enough to give anyone nightmares!

Nightmares – that wasn't such a bad
idea. Bertie slipped out of the room. A
cunning plan had started
to form in his head.

Thump, thump,
thump! Bertie
was banging on
the bathroom
door.
Bella opened up.
"What?"

"I need the toilet. You've been in there
hours!" complained Bertie.

Bella came out of the bathroom and
barged past him.

"Goodnight, Bella!" said Bertie sweetly.

"Huh," she grunted.

Dirty Bertie

"I hope you can sleep," said Bertie.

Bella stopped. She turned round. "Why shouldn't I sleep?"

"You mean Suzy didn't tell you?"

"Tell me what?" said Bella.

Bertie lowered his voice.

"That my room's haunted."

"Ha ha, very funny," said Bella.

"Why do you think I've been begging to sleep in Suzy's room?" said Bertie.

"You didn't beg, your mum made you."

Bertie shook his head. He glanced around. "It's the noises," he whispered. "They keep me awake."

"Noises?" said Bella.

"The bumps and thumps. The moans and groans," said Bertie.

"Oh," said Bella, turning rather pale.

"Still, some people don't hear them. It's only if you're scared of ghosts. You're not, are you?"

"Me?" said Bella. "Course not."

"That's OK then. Sweet dreams!"

Bertie closed his door and smiled to himself. *That ought to do it*, he thought.

Eleven o'clock. Bella was tossing and turning in her bed. She couldn't sleep.

Her mattress was too lumpy. The room was too dark. Worst of all, she kept imagining she heard strange noises. Of course Bertie had been making it up. Suzy said he was. There was no such thing as ghosts.

CREAK, CREAK, CREAK!

What was that? Bella held her breath.

THUMP, THUMP, THUMP!

It sounded like footsteps on the landing. Bella gripped the covers tightly.

"Suzy?" she hissed. "Suzy. Are you awake?"

There was no answer from the Z bed. RATTLE, RATTLE! went the door handle.

"EEEEEEEEEHHH!" went the door as it swung open by itself.

"Help!" whimpered Bella, diving under the covers. "Who's there?"

She peeped out. There it was! A ghost stumbling through the dark towards her.

"Woooooooh!" it moaned.
"Wooooooh!"

"Suzy," croaked Bella. "Suzy, wake up!"

"Woooooooooh," moaned the ghost.

Closer and closer it came. Bella could

see its bare white feet.

"You must leave this place!" it moaned. "Leave this … OUCH!"

A pillow had thwacked the ghost on the back of the head. Suzy yanked off the ghost's white sheet, revealing its blue pyjamas.

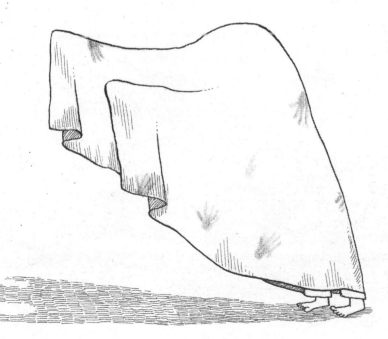

"BERTIE!" snarled Suzy.

"Um, hello," said Bertie.

"Get out," said Suzy. "Get out and don't come back."

"Or what?" said Bertie.

WHUMP! A pillow whacked Bertie in the face. THUMP! Another clouted him on the ear. Bertie fled from the room under a hail of blows.

"And next time I'm telling Mum!" Suzy called after him.

Bertie shut the door behind him. Trust his rotten sister to wake up and spoil everything. He would have to try plan B.

Midnight. The house was as quiet as the grave. Suzy was asleep. Bossy Bella was asleep. Bertie was not asleep. He was

creeping along the landing with
something in his hand. He opened his
bedroom door and stole inside. Now
where to hide? His eyes fell on the
windowsill above Bella's bed. Perfect!
Bella was talking in her sleep. "Get off.
It's my go," she mumbled.

Bertie peeped out from behind the
curtains. He brought out a big plastic
spider on a string. Slowly he began to
lower the spider towards his victim.
Lower and lower it dangled, spinning
round on its string. Bertie leaned out a
little further to get a better view. The
spider brushed Bella's hair. Bella's eyes
snapped open. They bulged with fear. A
giant black tarantula was inches from her
face. Its red eyes were staring at her. It
waggled its eight hairy legs.

Dirty Bertie

"ARGGHHHHHHHH!" screamed Bella.

Bertie was so startled he slipped off the windowsill and landed on top of Bella, who kicked and screamed.

"ARGH! GEROFFME! HEEEELP!"

The noise woke up Suzy.

"Muuuuuuum! Bertie's in our room!"

CLICK! The bedroom light came on. Mum stood in the doorway wrapped in her dressing gown.

"Bertie!" she seethed. "What do you think you're doing?"

"There was a huge black spider!" wailed Bella. "It was in my hair!"

Mum bent down. She picked the plastic spider off the floor and dangled it under Bertie's nose.

"Yours, I think," she said.

"Oh, um, thanks. I was looking for

that," said Bertie.

Mum glared at him. "Go to your room. And if I catch you out of bed one more time there'll be no sweets for a month."

Bertie trooped back to his room. He closed the door behind him and got into bed. Operation Ghost had failed. So had Operation Spider. He thought he better not try Operation Ants in the Pants. It looked like he'd be sleeping in Suzy's bed tonight after all.

CHAPTER 4

Meanwhile, in Bertie's bedroom, Bella was still awake. She wished Suzy's mum hadn't mentioned sweets. Thinking of sweets always made her hungry. She'd practically had nothing at all for supper.

At home she always kept a stash of sweets handy in case she got hungry at bedtime. Maybe Suzy's horrible little brother had some hidden somewhere?

Bella looked under the bed. Nothing there. She looked under the pillow. Nothing. She opened the bedside cupboard. On the shelf was a small plastic pot. Eagerly, Bella took it out and read the words scrawled on the side.

Ahaa! Sweeties! thought Bella.

She prised off the lid and peered inside.

A foul, putrid smell hit her like a force-ten gale. The pong of mouldy cabbage and rotten eggs filled the room. Bella clapped a hand to her mouth. She was going to be sick. She couldn't breathe.

"AHHHH! UGGGHHHHH!" she cried, dropping the stink bomb.

Suzy woke up.

"Bella! What are you
... EURGH! What's
that dreadful stink?"
she gasped.
"I'm dying!"
choked Bella. "I'm
suffocating! Let me
out!"

BANG! BANG! BANG!

Someone was hammering on Bertie's door.

Suzy and Bella burst in. "I need my bedroom back!" panted Suzy.

"What?" asked Bertie.

"It's horrible! It stinks! You've got to let us sleep in here!" begged Suzy.

"What are you talking about?"

"The smell – from that thing! It's choking us."

It dawned on Bertie – the stink bomb. He'd forgotten all about it.

"So you want me to give you back your bedroom?" he said slowly.

"Yes, yes. Please, Bertie! We can't sleep in there!" said Suzy.

"Hmmm," said Bertie. "I'll have to think about it."

"We'll do anything!" pleaded Bella.

Bertie raised his eyebrows. "Anything?"

Five minutes later Bertie was settled back in his own bed. True the room was a little whiffy, but he didn't really mind. Once you got used to it, the smell wasn't so bad – he couldn't see why the girls were making such a fuss. In any case all that mattered was he was back in his own room. And tomorrow Suzy and Bella had promised to play whatever he wanted. Bertie had already thought of a good game – it was called Pass the Stink Bomb.

WALKIES!

CHAPTER 1

"Dog training classes?" Bertie stared at his mum in horror.

"Yes. No arguments, please, Bertie," said Mum.

"But why do I have to go?"

"Because someone has to take Whiffer. He can't go on his own."

"Why can't you take him?" asked Bertie.

"I'm far too busy."

"What about Dad then?"

"Oh no," said Dad hastily. "I'm *really* busy. Anyway he's your dog."

"But he doesn't need training!" protested Bertie.

Mum snorted. "Bertie! He barks every time the doorbell goes."

"And he's always climbing on the sofa," grumbled Dad.

"He licks food off your plate," said Mum. "And last week he did a poo on Mrs Nicely's lawn."

"He's a dog," said Bertie. "That's what dogs do!"

"Well it's high time he learned to behave," said Mum firmly. "And I'm told this dog trainer can work wonders."

Bertie sighed. It wasn't fair. He didn't

want to take Whiffer to training classes.
He got quite enough classes at school.

"Anyway, he *is* trained," he argued. "I've
been training him for ages."

"Bertie, he does what he likes," said
Mum.

"Not always," said Bertie. "Sometimes
he listens to me."

Mum gave him one of her looks.
Whiffer was dozing on his cushion in the
corner. Bertie turned to him and
pointed.

"Stay, Whiffer," he ordered. "STAY!"

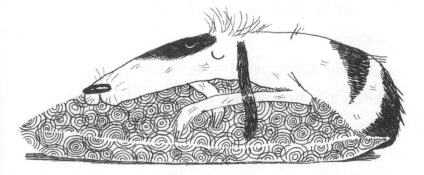

Whiffer opened one eye lazily then went on dozing.

"See?" said Bertie. "Like I said — he does what I say."

Mum folded her arms. "Very funny. You are taking him to classes and that is the end of it."

The following Friday evening Dad drove Bertie and Whiffer to the leisure centre.

In the big hall dogs of all shapes and sizes waited with their owners. Whiffer pulled at his lead and whined. He wanted to make friends.

The trainer was called Miss Bowser. She had wiry hair and a face like a bad-tempered bulldog. Bertie could see why animals would obey her.

Dirty Bertie

Miss Bowser clapped her hands and told everyone to line up for inspection.

"Mmm," she said, patting a red setter. "Good, good. Splendid."

When she came to Whiffer she stopped and clicked her tongue.

"And what have we here?"

"My dog," said Bertie.

"I can see it's a dog. I mean what is his *name*?"

"He's called Whiffer."

"Whiffer?" she barked. "That's an odd name for a dog."

"Well he can be pretty smelly, especially when you're watching TV," explained Bertie. "Sometimes he does one and the pong's so bad you can smell it upstairs."

"Good gracious!" said Miss Bowser, drawing back a little.

Dirty Bertie

"I don't think he can help it," said Bertie.

"He will LEARN to help it," Miss Bowser replied, grimly. "In my classes dogs do what they are told." She eyed Whiffer and raised a stern finger.

"SIT!" she ordered.

Whiffer sat. Bertie was amazed. He'd never done that for anyone before.

CHAPTER 2

The class began. Miss Bowser handed out dog biscuits.

"Treats must be earned," she told her class. "A naughty dog does not get a treat. Let's begin with a simple command. Teaching your dog to come when called."

Bertie groaned. He'd tried a million times

to get Whiffer to come. The only time
he came was when his dog bowl was full.

"Step away from your dog and turn to
face them," instructed Miss Bowser.

Bertie walked away from Whiffer.
When he turned round, Whiffer was
right behind him, wagging his tail. He
could smell dog biscuits.

"No, Whiffer. You stay over there," said
Bertie. "You come when I say 'Come',
OK?"

Whiffer licked his hand and tried to
nose in Bertie's pockets. Bertie dragged
him back to his place by the collar.

"Now call your dog by name," said
Miss Bowser. "When he comes give him
a treat. And remember, heaps and heaps
of praise."

"Whiffer! Come, boy!" called Bertie.

Whiffer looked the other way.

"Come, boy. Come! COME!" yelled Bertie.

Whiffer was the only dog in the hall who hadn't moved. The other owners cooed and fussed over their dogs, who were wolfing down their biscuits. Miss Bowser strode over to Bertie.

"Where is your treat?" she boomed.

"Um, in my pocket."

"No, no, you have to let him see it! Give it to me!"

Miss Bowser held out her hand with the dog biscuit. Whiffer barked and flew at her – a whirlwind of fur and legs and tongue.

Miss Bowser found herself pinned to the floor, with Whiffer on top of her, crunching his biscuit happily.

Dirty Bertie

"How did it go?" asked Mum when Bertie got home later that evening.

"It was terrible," groaned Bertie, slumping into a chair. "It's worse than school."

Whiffer padded over to his cushion and flopped down wearily.

"Never mind," said Mum. "It's only the first lesson. I'm sure it will get better."

"You haven't met Miss Bowser," said Bertie darkly. "She shouts all the time – even when she's standing right next to you. I bet she used to be in the army. I bet she got tired of shouting at soldiers all day and decided she'd get a job shouting at dogs and their owners."

"As long as Whiffer does what he's told I don't mind," said Mum.

Dirty Bertie

"That's just it, he doesn't!" moaned Bertie. "He gets mixed up. He sits when he's meant to come and when I say 'Walkies', he lies down! The only thing he's good at is stuffing himself with biscuits!"

Mum glanced at Whiffer, who had dozed off to sleep. "Well there's seven more weeks, he's bound to improve."

"Seven?" Bertie groaned. Seven more weeks of Miss Bowser shouting and Whiffer coming bottom of the class. He didn't know if he could stand it.

"And you didn't tell me there'd be a test," he grumbled. "Whiffer's got to pass his ODD."

"His what?" asked Mum.

"ODD. Obedient Dog Diploma," said

Bertie. "That's what she gives you."

"Good," said Mum. "With what it's costing me I'll expect him to pass."

Bertie looked doubtful. "Well," he said. "I wouldn't bet on it."

Mum had an idea. "How about this?" she said. "I'll offer you a reward. If Whiffer passes I will double your pocket money."

Bertie looked up. "Really?"

"Really."

Bertie did a quick calculation. Double pocket money that would be … um … double what he usually got, which came to quite a lot. He could buy loads of things with twice the pocket money.

There was just one major problem. There was more chance of Whiffer passing his *driving test* than his Dog Diploma.

CHAPTER 3

Every week for the next six weeks
Bertie dragged Whiffer along to Miss
Bowser's classes. Whiffer showed no
signs of progress. He made friends with
a boxer called Bonzo. He learned to
steal biscuits from Bertie's pocket. But
he didn't learn to obey. Bertie was in
despair. At school he explained the

problem to Donna. Donna had a
hamster and a goldfish so she knew
about pets. She suggested they take
Whiffer to the park for extra lessons.

"It's no use," moaned Bertie, after
Whiffer had gone charging off for the
umpteenth time. "Let's face it, he's never
going to pass."

"Maybe you're just doing it wrong,"
said Donna.

"How can I be? I'm shouting just like
she does."

Whiffer came racing up. He'd
found a mangy old rubber ball
in the grass.

"Try one more time. Tell him
to sit," said Donna.

"SIT!" yelled Bertie.

"WHIFFER, SIT!"

Whiffer dropped the ball at Bertie's feet and barked. Bertie flopped down on the grass. Whiffer sat down too. Donna looked thoughtful.

"Let's try something else. I'll go over there and you come when I call you."

"Me?" said Bertie. "It's not me we're meant to be training!"

Donna looked at him. "Do you want my help or not?"

Bertie sighed. Donna could be very bossy when she wanted to be.

"Ready?" said Donna. "OK. Come!" Bertie walked over to her and Whiffer trotted behind. Donna looked pleased.

"Now roll over," she said.

"Who?"

"You! Go on, do it!"

Feeling pretty stupid, Bertie lay down

and rolled over. Whiffer barked joyfully
and rolled over too. This was a great
game.

"See! I was right," laughed Donna. "He
does whatever you do. All you have to
do is get him to copy you!"

"Wow!" said Bertie. "You're a genius!"

"I know," said Donna, modestly.

Bertie still looked worried. "But what
about the test?" he asked. "It's not just
rolling over, there'll be tunnels and fences
and stuff."

"Easy!" shrugged Donna. "You just do
it with him. Trust me. It'll work."

The following Friday Miss Bowser's class
gathered for their final exam. Bertie eyed
the other dogs – Bonzo the boxer, Trixie

Dirty Bertie

the terrier and Dodie the Dalmatian. They had all been washed and combed for their big day.

Out in the park was a doggy obstacle course. There were tiny hurdles, poles to weave through and a long blue tunnel. Miss Bowser had her clipboard and pencil at the ready to mark each dog's performance. Whiffer tugged at his lead. Over on the other side of the park he'd spotted some boys playing frisbee. Frisbee was his favourite game.

Dodie was first to be tested. She scored top marks, 10 out of 10 with no refusals. Bertie watched Bonzo and Trixie complete the course with flying colours too.

Whiffer didn't seem to be paying attention. He kept staring across the park.

Finally it was Bertie's turn. "OK, Whiffer," he whispered. "Just follow me." He set off at a run and cleared the first hurdle.

Miss Bowser waved her clipboard. "No, no, Bertie! The dog, not you!"

But Donna's plan was working. Whiffer copied Bertie, stepping over the hurdles and clearing the jump like a racehorse. Bertie got down on his hands and knees to crawl through the tunnel.

He danced in and out of the poles as everyone watched in amazement. Almost there! Suddenly a red frisbee whizzed by and hit him on the head.

Whiffer barked excitedly. A frisbee meant a game. *Uh oh*, thought Bertie and grabbed it before Whiffer could pounce. A boy in a football shirt ran up.

"Hey! That's ours!" he said.

Bertie meant to throw it back, but like most frisbees this one had a mind of its own. It took off and curved back over his head. It zoomed over the line of waiting dogs like a low-flying jet. Fifteen pairs of eyes watched it go. Fifteen dogs barked and leaped in the air, straining at their leads. Whiffer saw the frisbee coming back his way. He leaped high, caught it in his mouth and set off like a greyhound. Before you could shout "Stay!" the other dogs were after him.

"Yikes!" cried Bertie, dodging out of the way as the pack thundered past. Dogs flattened Miss Bowser's hurdles. Dogs swarmed like rats through the blue tunnel. Miss Bowser tried to stop them. She held up her hand like a policeman stopping the traffic. "SIT!" she yelled. Bonzo leaped at her and she vanished in the scrum.

CHAPTER 4

It took some time for all the dogs to be rounded up. The frisbee was returned to its owners slightly chewed at the edges. The blue tunnel had somehow got ripped. But what Bertie didn't understand was why everyone blamed him!

"It wasn't my frisbee!" he pointed out.

"I could've been killed getting bashed on the head like that. Instead of blaming me, you should be asking if I'm all right!"

Miss Bowser did not seem to care if Bertie was all right. She had grass in her hair and muddy paw prints all over her skirt. She said they would get on with the awards so everyone could go home.

Bertie watched gloomily as each dog and his owner went forward. He doubted if Whiffer would be getting his Diploma, not after all the fuss there'd been.

"And finally…" said Miss Bowser. "Bertie and Whiffer."

Bertie trooped out to the front. Miss Bowser glared at him.

"In twenty years I have never met a dog I couldn't train," she said. "Until now."

She lowered her voice. "However, I

will give you this on one condition. That
you promise you will never ever come
to one of my classes again."

"Oh, I won't," said Bertie. "Honestly."

"Very well," said Miss Bowser, handing
him a piece of paper.

Bertie looked at it.

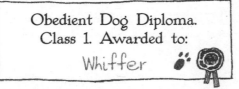

Obedient Dog Diploma.
Class 1. Awarded to:
Whiffer

"Wow! Thanks!" he said. "Look,
Whiffer. You passed!"

Ten minutes later Bertie ran over to
the car park where his mum was waiting.

"Look, Mum!" he cried. "We did it!
Whiffer passed!"

Mum was delighted. She handed
Bertie his pocket money – double his
usual amount. "Well done, Bertie. And

clever old Whiffer, I told you he could do it!" She glanced behind Bertie. "Where is he, by the way?"

Bertie looked round just in time to catch sight of Whiffer racing across the field. He called out to him.

"Whiffer! Here, boy! Come!"

Whiffer didn't even look back.

Obedient Dog Diploma.
Class 1. Awarded to:
Whiffer

For Sarah and Paul – I haven't danced to
Culture Club since 1984! ~ D R
For the fab Frosties ~ A M

Contents

YUCK!

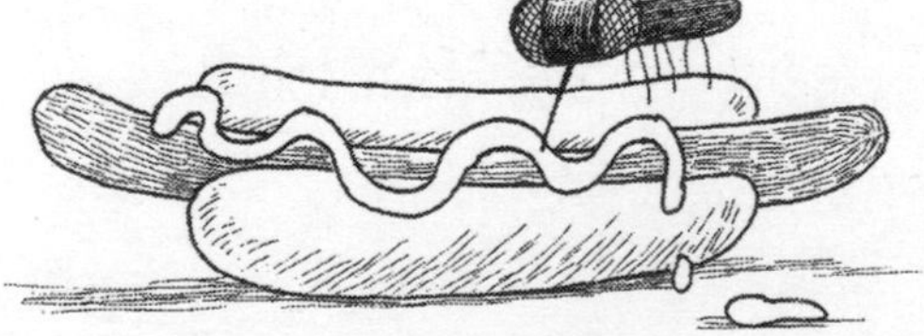

CHAPTER 1

Bertie dumped his bag and coat in the hall and burst into the kitchen. His mum was writing a letter.

"Mum! Guess what?"

"Hello, Bertie!" said Mum. "How was school?"

"Oh, the same," said Bertie. "But Mum, you'll never guess what…"

"Probably not," said Mum, going back to her letter.

"There's a fair tomorrow night!" cried Bertie, excitedly. He waited for his mum to jump up and turn cartwheels. But she just said "Mmm" and went on writing.

"A funfair, Mum, with rides and prizes and everything!"

"Yes, you said."

"So can I go? Tomorrow night. Please Mum, can I?" Bertie was hopping from foot to foot as if he needed the toilet.

Mum looked up. "No, Bertie. I don't think so."

Bertie's mouth dropped open. "But … but why not?"

"Because I said so. I took you to the funfair last year and I remember what happened."

Dirty Bertie

Bertie cast his mind back to last year. True, he'd nagged his mum all night to go on the ghost train – then screamed to get off. True, he'd fallen in the watersplash trying to rescue his toffee apple, but that could have happened to anyone.

"But Mum!" he begged. "All my friends will be going."

"Bertie, I said no. No means no."

Dirty Bertie

Dad was in the garden raking the lawn.

"Dad!" cried Bertie, rushing outside.

"Bertie, I just swept that up."

"What?"

Dad groaned. "That pile of grass you've just trampled through."

"Oh, sorry." Bertie looked at his shoes. If people left piles of grass lying around how was he meant to avoid them?

"Dad," he said. "Can you take me to

the funfair tomorrow night?"

"No," said Dad.

"Why not?"

"I've got choir practice."

"But it's only on for one night."

"Sorry, Bertie. Ask your mum."

"I did. She won't take me either."

"Then you can't go."

"But … but … arghh!" Bertie stomped off, trailing grass all through the house.

Dirty Bertie

It wasn't fair. Why did he have such mean, selfish parents? They were always dragging him off to places he didn't want to go – like the dentist's or the countryside. But when it came to something important – like a funfair – they always said 'No'. Surely there was someone who could take him?

Of course! Gran! Gran was never too busy to do things with Bertie. She'd probably be grateful he asked her!

CHAPTER 2

DING DONG!

Gran opened the door.

"Oh, hello Bertie, come in. I was just talking about you!"

Gran was watching telly with her neighbour, Sherry. Bertie had met Sherry before. Generally he did his best to avoid her.

Dirty Bertie

"Hello Bertie! Come and give your Auntie Sherry a big kiss."

Bertie screwed up his face as Sherry planted a lipsticky kiss on his cheek. "Well!" she said. "Isn't he growing up fast?"

"I know," said Gran.

"Next thing you know he'll be coming round with his girlfriend!"

Bertie turned crimson. *Girlfriend?* He'd rather bring his pet tarantula!

"Gran," he said. "Are you doing anything tomorrow night?"

"Tomorrow? No, I don't think so."

"Only I was thinking maybe you'd like to take me to the funfair."

"The funfair!" said Gran. "Goodness, it's ages since I went to one of those."

"I love a good funfair," said Sherry, helping herself to a slice of cake.

"So can you take me?" said Bertie. "Tomorrow night? Can you?"

"I don't see why not," said Gran. "Maybe Sherry would like to come, too?"

"What a good idea!" said Sherry. "We'll make a party of it. Won't that be fun, Bertie?"

"Oh … er yes," said Bertie. If he could go to the fair he'd put up with anyone – even Sherry.

CHAPTER 3

Saturday night arrived. The funfair was lit up like a Christmas tree. Bertie breathed in the sweet smell of candyfloss. Music boomed and thumped. The ghost train wailed. People on the rollercoaster screamed. *This is going to be brilliant,* thought Bertie. No mean parents to tell him what to do. He could hardly wait!

They pushed their way through the crowds, looking at all the rides.

"Oooh," said Sherry, "I don't know where to start."

Bertie stopped. At one of the stalls was a sign in big red letters:

TRY YOUR LUCK! WIN A PRIZE!

His eyes lit up. In the middle of all the plastic watches and droopy dollies was the biggest jar of sweets he'd ever seen.

It was full to bursting with lollypops, toffees, chews and chocolates. Bertie reckoned there had to be at least a thousand sweets in there – enough to last him a whole week!

All you had to do was throw a hoop and land it over the jar.

Dirty Bertie

"Gran, can I have a go? Can I, please, can I?" Bertie begged.

"Of course, dear." Gran got out her purse and paid the Hoopla man. The best thing about Gran was she hardly ever said 'No'.

Bertie took careful aim. His first hoop fell way short. His second skimmed off the Hoopla man's head. His third hit the sweet jar with a plunk! and pinged off.

Dirty Bertie

"Oh, bad luck, Bertie!" said Sherry. "Let me have a try."

Gran and Sherry both tried their luck. Sherry won a prize — but not the jar of sweets Bertie had been hoping for. Instead she won two sets of Deely Boppers. Sherry put one on. They wobbled around on her head crazily, flashing red and green.

"You try them, Dotty," she giggled. "I bet they'd suit you."

Gran put on the other pair and they both doubled up, hooting with laughter.

"What do you think, Bertie?" they asked, posing arm in arm.

"Um, great," said Bertie. "But aren't you a bit, you know, old for them?"

"Ooh look! He's gone all pink!" giggled Sherry. "Are we embarrassing you, Bertie?"

Bertie trailed behind Gran and Sherry, watching their Deely Boppers bob up and down like yo-yos. This wasn't what he'd planned at all.

In fact, he was starting to think this could turn into the worst night of his life. He seemed to be stuck with two alien grannies from the Planet Bonkers. What if someone from his class saw him? He'd never live it down.

Suddenly he stopped in his tracks. Climbing off the roundabout was a pale, smug-faced boy, holding a balloon. It was his sworn enemy, Know-All Nick.

Bertie looked around in desperation. He couldn't be seen with two mad grannies wearing disco lights. He had to escape!

Quickly, he grabbed Gran by the arm and steered her in the opposite direction.

"Where are we going now?" asked Sherry, hurrying after them.

"Look, bumper cars!" pointed Gran. "Bagsy I drive!"

Gran bought three tokens from the lady in the booth.

"Couldn't I go by myself?" pleaded Bertie.

"Don't be silly," scoffed Gran. "It's no fun on your own."

Gran dragged him over to a bright red bumper car and the three of them squashed in. He could see people pointing them out and laughing. He slid down in his seat, trying to hide.

The music started and Gran's foot slammed down on the pedal. The car lurched away.

BUMP! They crashed into the yellow car in front.

THUD! They swerved left and rammed a silver car.

"Ha ha! Got you!" yelled Gran. She wrenched the steering wheel round and they went into a spin before zipping off again.

"You're going the wrong way!" cried Bertie, pointing at the cars heading towards them like a swarm of bees.

"Rubbish!" said Gran. "They're going the wrong way."

BUMP! CRASH! WHAM!

A dozen bumper cars slammed into each other and shuddered to a halt.

Arguments broke out as the drivers tried to reverse and thudded into each other. One of the attendants waded in to try and calm everyone down. Bertie meanwhile had spotted a boy with a balloon waiting with his dad. He sank even lower in his seat. It was Know-All Nick.

"Bertie!" said Gran. "What are you doing down there?"

CHAPTER 4

Bertie bit into a hot dog and tried to think. Somehow he had to get away from the grannies before they ran into Nick again. They passed a ride called Rattle and Roll. A sign in big letters said:

> ## WARNING!
> THIS RIDE NOT SUITABLE FOR UNDER 7'S,
> OVER 70'S OR NERVOUS NINNIES.

Dirty Bertie

Bertie suddenly had a brilliant idea.
All he had to do was pick all the scariest
rides in the fair. Everyone knew grannies
hated scary rides. They could go off and
have a quiet cup of tea while Bertie
enjoyed himself.

"What's next then,
Bertie?" asked Gran.

"This one!" pointed
Bertie.

"Heavens!" said Gran.
"Rattle and Roll?"

Sherry looked up at the gigantic tower. "I dare you, Dotty," she said.

Gran's eyes twinkled. "I double dare you back," she said.

Bertie stared at them. "But … won't you be scared?" he asked.

"Of course we will," laughed Gran.

"I'll probably scream my head off," giggled Sherry.

"Me too," said Gran. "But Bertie can hold my hand."

Bertie took his seat between Gran and Sherry. The safety bar clunked into place.

GRUNT! SNORT! The machine sounded like a dragon. They began to rise slowly into the air. Higher and higher. Bertie tried not to look down.

"This isn't that scary," he said.

SNORT! WHOOSH! They shot

earthwards at a million miles an hour.

Gran screamed. Sherry shrieked.

Bertie hung on for dear life.

UP they shot. Then DOWN.

UP. DOWN. DOWN. UP. DOWN.

Bertie clutched at his stomach.

Finally the ride stopped and the bar
went up.

"Woo! That was amazing!" whooped
Sherry, as they got off.

"I've come over all giddy!" gasped
Gran. "Are you all right, Bertie? You've
gone a bit pale."

"URRRRRR!" groaned Bertie.

They queued at one of the food kiosks.
By the time they reached the front
Bertie wasn't feeling quite so dizzy. He
couldn't decide between candyfloss or a
toffee apple or a fizzy drink – so he had
all three.

Holding everything at once proved a
bit tricky. He tried putting the candyfloss
in his pocket to eat his toffee apple, but

Dirty Bertie

it got stuck to his trousers. When he
pulled it off it somehow fell on the floor.

"Ugh! That's dirty, Bertie. You can't eat
that!" said Gran.

"Why not?" said Bertie. "It's only a bit
of grass." He picked off an ant and took
a big mouthful. "Want shum?" he asked.

"Er, no thanks, you have it," said Gran.

Dirty Bertie

Turning a corner, Bertie screeched to a halt. Know-All Nick had just arrived at the bottom of the helter skelter. Bertie looked around desperately for somewhere to hide. Any moment now Nick would spot them and come over.

He ducked under a barrier and joined a queue for one of the rides.

"Goodness!" said Gran. "Are you sure?"

"What?" said Bertie, looking up. He gulped. The sign said:

MIGHTY MEGAMAX
THE WORLD'S FASTEST ROLLERCOASTER.

Bertie had never been on a rollercoaster before. To tell the truth he wasn't sure he wanted to. But it was too late, they'd reached the front and Gran was paying for the tickets.

Dirty Bertie

RUMBLE, RUMBLE, RUMBLE!

Bertie clung to the safety bar as their carriage climbed the steep track. The rollercoaster looked scarier than Miss Boot on a Monday morning. When he glanced down his stomach gave a lurch.

Maybe all that candyfloss wasn't such a good idea. He felt sick. He felt dizzy. He wanted to get off.

Dirty Bertie

The carriage reached the crest of the hill and Bertie gaped at the drop below.
ARRRRRRGGHHHHHHH!

They were hurtling towards the ground at the speed of light. He was going to die. They were all going to die.

"WHEEE!" whooped Gran and Sherry. "This is fun!"

Five terrifying minutes later the carriage slowed to a halt. Bertie staggered out. His hair stuck out like a hedgehog. His legs had turned to jelly. His face was a pale green.

"Hello, Bertie!" jeered a voice. "Enjoy your ride?"

Know-All Nick was waiting by the barrier, and he was holding something large and shiny.

"Look what I won on the hoopla!" he boasted.

Bertie stared at the giant sweet jar stuffed with lollipops, chocolates and chews. His stomach heaved. He was going to be…

BLEUUUGHHHHH!

CHAPTER 1

"Don't you look smart!" beamed Mum.
"Come and look in the mirror."

Bertie plodded into the hall and
scowled at his reflection. He was
wearing a sailor suit. It was Victorian
History Day at school and everyone was
supposed to come in costume. Mum had
found the sailor suit in a charity shop.

Dirty Bertie

Bertie thought it was the drippiest thing he'd ever seen. The white trousers flapped above his ankles. The shirt had a stupid floppy collar. The hat had a wobbly blue pompom.

"There! What do you think?" asked Mum.

Bertie pulled a face. "I look like a girl," he said.

"Bertie, that's what boys used to wear in those days. I think you look very smart."

"Can't I go as a pirate? I've got the eyepatch and everything."

"It's Victorian Day," sighed Mum. "They didn't have pirates."

"A dustman then?" said Bertie.

"No!"

"Or a robber? I bet they had robbers."

"Bertie," said Mum. "I went to a lot of trouble to find you this costume and you're going to wear it. Now hurry up and get ready."

Bertie stomped up the stairs to look for his shoes. *It's not fair*, he thought. Why were parents always telling you what to wear? He didn't go round telling them what to wear!

Dirty Bertie

In his bedroom Bertie stared gloomily at himself in the wardrobe mirror. All his friends would have much better costumes than him. Donna was going as a flower girl and Eugene as a butler. Darren had said he was coming as a chimney sweep, which Bertie wished he'd thought of himself. All *he* had was a sailor suit with a stupid collar and a silly pompom. Maybe if he got rid of the collar the shirt wouldn't look so bad?

RIPPPP!

Dirty Bertie

Uh oh – he seemed to have torn it.
Now the collar was hanging loose on
one side. His mum would have a fit if
she saw it. He yanked at the other side
to even it up.

RIPPPPPP!

Yikes!
That had
only made
things
worse. The
collar had

come off but the shirt had a big rip in it.
Now he looked like a scruffy old beggar.

Bertie stared. What a brilliant idea! He
could go as a beggar! In Victorian times
there were millions of beggars. You could
hardly walk down the street without
tripping over one. And he wouldn't even

have to change his costume. All it
needed was a few small alterations. Now
where did Mum keep the scissors?

"Bertie!" Mum shouted. "What are you
doing up there? You're going to be late!"
"Coming!" said Bertie. He thumped

downstairs and
landed in the
hall.

Mum stared in
horror. "Bertie!
What have you
done?"

"It's my
costume!" said
Bertie. "I'm a
beggar!"

Dirty Bertie

Bertie was still wearing his sailor suit, or what was left of it. The sleeves hung in tatters. The white trousers looked like they'd been attacked by killer moths. (Bertie had got a little carried away with the scissors.) Bertie's feet were bare and he was wearing a scruffy old cap on his head.

Mum leaned heavily against the front door. "How did this happen?" she groaned.

"I did it myself," beamed Bertie.

"I can see that. You've completely ruined your costume!"

Bertie shrugged. "Beggars don't wear sailor suits," he said. "They have to look poor. If they went round in sailor suits no one would give them any money."

Mum peered at him closely.

Dirty Bertie

"What's that on your face?"

"Dirt," said Bertie.

"No, those red blotches. You look like you've got measles."

"Oh yes," said Bertie. "Poor people were always getting plagues and diseases, we did it in school. Don't worry it's only felt pen, it'll probably come off."

Dirty Bertie

Mum passed a hand over her eyes.

"Bertie, please! You can't go to school like that."

"Why not?" asked Bertie. "Miss Boot said to come as a Victorian, so I am. I'm coming as a beggar."

"But you look like a scarecrow."

"That's how beggars look," said Bertie. "No one said anything about having to be smart."

Mum looked at her watch. They were late already.

CHAPTER 2

The Victorian Day turned out to be a bit
of a disappointment. Bertie had been
hoping they might play some Victorian
games or try some Victorian sweets, but
Miss Boot had other ideas. To get into
the spirit of the day she had brought a
cane. She made them sit in rows and
practise their handwriting in silence.

Dirty Bertie

If anyone spoke or laughed or burped
they had to go and stand in the corner.
Bertie spent quite a lot of time in the
corner.

Dirty Bertie

After school Mum collected him and
they stopped off at the supermarket.
Bertie usually liked helping with the
shopping. If he pushed the trolley and
didn't bash into anyone, Mum let him
have chocolate cake at the cafe. But
today they had Whiffer with them.

"Sorry," said Mum. "He'll have to wait
out here."

"Why?" asked Bertie.

Mum pointed at a sign by the door.
It said 'NO DOGS ALLOWED' in big
red letters.

Whiffer whined and wagged his tail at
Bertie.

"I'll stay with him," said Bertie. "He
gets lonely on his own."

Dirty Bertie

"All right," said Mum. "But don't go anywhere. And Bertie…"

"What?"

"Please take off that horrible hat."

Bertie took off his hat and sat down beside Whiffer. Whiffer rested his head in Bertie's lap and closed his eyes.

Shoppers passing by glanced down at the ragged, dirty-faced boy and his dog, sitting on the pavement. Some of them tutted to themselves while others shook their heads and gave him pitying looks. Bertie didn't notice people were staring – he was busy checking Whiffer's fur for fleas.

Suddenly a woman bent down, smiled and dropped a fifty pence coin into his hat.

Bertie looked up in surprise. People didn't usually give him money. At least not total strangers. Did they think he was begging or something?

Dirty Bertie

He looked down at his ragged clothes and muddy shoes. Of course, he was still dressed as a beggar! The woman must have thought his hat was there to collect money! Bertie was thrilled. *This is fantastic!* he thought. *I bet Eugene doesn't get mistaken for a real butler!*

Wait till he told his friends about this tomorrow! His costume was even better than he thought.

Bertie tried out his sad face, waiting for someone else to pass by.

It worked. The next person, a man in a smart coat, dropped twenty pence into his hat. Fifty plus twenty that made um … seventy pence already! At this rate he would be rich – and all he had to do was sit on the pavement looking sorry for himself.

CHAPTER 3

For the next fifteen minutes, Bertie tried
out different expressions on the shoppers
passing by. Smiling, he found, was no use
at all. It was better to look as if your pet
earthworm had just died. Some shoppers
hurried on past without paying any
attention, but several stopped and soon
Bertie's hat was filling up with shiny coins.

He was just about to count what he'd earned, when a woman stopped in front of him. She was wearing a brown fur coat and a matching hat.

"You poor child," she tutted. "Where is your mother?"

"Oh, she's not here," stammered Bertie, putting on his sad face.

"You mean she's just left you by yourself? Is she coming back?"

"Well ... I expect so," said Bertie, glancing towards the supermarket. "I expect she'll be back later." (He hoped it would be much later.)

"And does she know you are — begging?" asked the woman.

"Oh yes, it's okay, she doesn't mind," said Bertie. "She wants me to beg."

"Good heavens!" said the woman, sounding horrified. "Are you saying she forces you to do this?"

"Oh no, not forces me no, but if I don't do any begging we won't get any supper," said Bertie. "Cos my family are very, very poor. Poor as anything. My dad's actually a chimney sweep," he added by way of explanation.

The woman bent closer. She stared at the ugly red blotches on Bertie's face.

"You poor boy. How long have you been living like this? You don't look well at all," she murmured.

"I'm okay, really," said Bertie. "It's probably just a bit of plague or something."

The woman quickly took a step back. "You stay there," she said. "Stay there while I go and fetch someone."

Bertie waited till the woman had gone into the supermarket. He felt it would be wise to disappear before she came back. Whoever she had gone to fetch it could only lead to trouble. He picked up his hatful of coins. But, just at that moment, the woman reappeared from an exit to his left. She was followed by a tall security guard in a brown uniform.

Dirty Bertie

They were both marching towards him
with a determined look. Bertie did the
only thing he could think of. He fled.
Jamming his hat on to his head, he
darted into the supermarket with
Whiffer at his heels.

"Hey!" cried the guard. "Come back!"

CHAPTER 4

Bertie looked around, desperate for
somewhere to hide. People were staring
at his ragged clothes and tutting at the
sight of Whiffer. In his panic he'd
forgotten that dogs weren't allowed in
the supermarket. As he dithered, the
guard appeared in the doorway and
spotted him. "Hey!" he cried.

Dirty Bertie

Grabbing the nearest trolley, Bertie picked up Whiffer and plonked him in the basket. Then he set off at top speed, pushing the trolley in front of him.

"You! Wait! Come back!" cried the guard, chasing after him.

Bertie didn't stop to explain. He raced down the fruit aisle, scattering startled shoppers in his path. "Sorry! Sorry! Can't stop!" he panted.

A woman stepped out in front of him and froze with a pineapple in her hands.

At the last moment, Bertie swerved round her and skidded past the cheese counter. Glancing back, he caught sight of the guard puffing after him. He sped down the next aisle, narrowly missing a tower of toilet rolls. Whiffer was standing up in the trolley barking excitedly.

Dirty Bertie

Bertie looked up just in time to see a trolley parked across the aisle, blocking his way. The owner was reaching up to a shelf for a box of eggs. Her mouth fell open when she saw Bertie hurtling towards her. It was Mum.

Bertie tried to slam on the brakes, but the trolley didn't seem to have any.

CRASH!

Whiffer went flying through the air and landed in Mum's arms. Mum's shopping went flying, too. A dozen eggs hit the floor with a crunch, followed by a pint of milk and a shower of cornflakes.

"Bertie!" cried Mum. "What on earth…"

Bertie was about to explain, when the security guard caught up with them. He stood panting for breath as the lady in the fur coat appeared, along with a small crowd keen to see what all the fuss was about. Mum sat in a pool of milk, staring at Bertie.

"Is this your son?" demanded the guard.

"I'm afraid so," said Mum, turning a little pink. "We'll pay for any damage."

"Never mind that," said the guard. "There's a law against it."

"You should be ashamed of yourself!" interrupted the lady.

"Me?" said Mum.

"Sending a boy of his age out on the streets to beg," said the lady. "I've a good mind to report you!"

"I'm sorry, I don't know what you're talking about," said Mum.

"Begging!" said the lady.

"Begging?" said Mum. She looked at Bertie. "Oh, I see! I'm afraid you've made a mistake. He's only dressed like that for school. He wasn't actually begging, were you, Bertie?"

There was an awkward silence as everyone looked at Bertie.

Dirty Bertie

He pulled off his hat, hoping he might look more sorry without it.

A shower of coins tumbled out and hit the floor, running in all directions.

"Um," said Bertie. "I can explain…"

CHAPTER 1

Mum put down the phone. "Isn't that nice," she said. "Simon and Jenny have invited us all to go and stay next weekend."

Dad groaned. Suzy pulled a face. Bertie paused with a spoonful of soggy cereal halfway to his mouth.

"Who are Simon and Jenny?" he asked.

"You remember, they came to visit us at Easter – with baby Molly."

The cereal dropped off Bertie's spoon and splatted on the table.

"Not them?" he said.

"Yes, them – and please don't wipe that up with your sleeve."

"But I don't have to go, do I?"

"Well of course you do, Bertie. We're all invited. And Simon and Jenny are our friends."

"They're not my friends," said Bertie.

Dirty Bertie

"Well Jenny is my friend, I've known her since we were at school," said Mum. "Anyway, when people invite you to stay it's rude not to accept."

"It'll be boring. There'll be nothing for me to do!" grumbled Bertie.

"Of course there will. You can play with Molly. She likes you – remember?"

Bertie wasn't likely to forget. Molly was Simon and Jenny's little girl – a podgy baby with a mass of golden curls. She had stuck to Bertie like glue all day, crying whenever he went out of the room.

She had sat on his lap and pulled his hair. She'd poked him in the eye and wanted to kiss him.

Suzy looked up from her homework.

"Mum, you know I'm at Nisha's next weekend? We're going riding."

"I know," said Mum. "So it'll just be the three of us."

Bertie's sister grinned and stuck out her tongue at him.

Bertie was speechless. "That's not FAIR! Why does she get out of it when I have to go?"

"Because Suzy is busy. It's been arranged for weeks."

"I'm busy, too!"

"You're not, Bertie."

"I might be. I might be doing something important."

"Like what?"

"Well, like…" Bertie looked around for inspiration. "…Like staying here to look after Whiffer. Someone's got to."

"I don't mind doing it," offered Dad.

"I thought of it first!" said Bertie.

"Gran will take care of Whiffer," said Mum. "We are spending the weekend with Simon and Jenny. And Bertie, I will expect you to be on your best behaviour."

Bertie slumped back in his chair, miserably. A whole weekend of Soppy Simon, Drippy Jenny and baby Molly. He dropped his spoon in his bowl and watched it sink beneath a sea of brown goo.

CHAPTER 2

DING DONG! Simon and Jenny threw open the door. "Come in!" they cried. Jenny had Molly in her arms. "Look Molly," she cooed. "Who's this come to see you? Who's this?"

"Bee bee! Da da da!" cried Molly, reaching out her chubby little arms.

"That's right, it's Bertie! Clever girl!"

nodded Jenny, beaming. "Show Bertie what you can do!"

Jenny set Molly down on the floor. Last time Bertie had seen her she had been crawling around on all fours. Now she tottered down the hall on her dumpy little legs, looking back to check they were watching.

"Walking? Goodness! Aren't you clever, Molly?" said Mum, clapping her hands.

"Isn't it amazing?" said Jenny, beaming with pride.

"Amazing!" nodded Simon.

Mum gave Dad a dig in the ribs.

"Oh yes, great," said Dad. "How long has she been – you know – walking?"

"Three weeks, two days," replied Simon. "I was in the kitchen the day it happened. Molly was sitting just there by the fridge, playing with her bricks. The next thing I knew she'd pulled herself up and just started walking. Didn't you, poppet? Yes you did, clever girl!"

Bertie caught Dad's eye. Were they going to be listening to this baby stuff all weekend? All this fuss over walking a few steps! Bertie walked miles to school and back every day and no one even seemed to notice!

Dirty Bertie

Molly had toddled into the lounge and came back clutching a small blue teddy. She held it out to Bertie, practically pushing it up his nose.

"Bee bee!" she said. "Da da da!"

"Oh, sweet! She wants you to have teddy!" said Jenny.

"Bertie have teddy? Bertie look after him?" asked Simon.

Bertie took the teddy. It had one chewed ear and its face was soggy with dribble.

"Say thank you, Bertie," prompted Mum.

"Oh right. Thanks," said Bertie, holding the teddy as far away as possible. Molly toddled up to him and hugged him round the waist.

"Oh look!" said Mum. "She likes you, Bertie."

Molly tilted back her head and presented her lips. Her nose was runny.

"Molly want a kiss? Kiss for Bertie?" said Jenny.

There was no escape. Bertie bent down and allowed Molly to plant a big slobbery kiss on his mouth. It was worse than being licked by Whiffer. Molly giggled. She wanted to do it again. And again. And again.

It was going to be a long weekend.

Dirty Bertie

175

Dirty Bertie

While the parents drank coffee, Molly dragged Bertie off to the playroom. He spent an hour making towers of building blocks so she could knock them down.

At five o'clock they gathered round the kitchen table to watch Molly having her supper. Jenny fed her spoonfuls of gloopy mush the colour of snot. Bertie thought it was hardly surprising that Molly spat most of it out.

"She's trying so hard," Jenny was saying. "Simon and I think she'll be talking any day now, don't we, sweetie?"

"Yes we do, sweetie," cooed Simon.

"Goodness," said Mum. "Bertie didn't start talking until he was almost two. How old is Molly now?"

Dirty Bertie

"Fourteen months," said Jenny. "It's still very young, but she's so advanced. Say 'Mum', Molly. Mum, mum, mum."

"Bee bee!" shouted Molly, banging her spoon. There was green mush all over her face and even a splodge in her hair. Bertie could hardly bear to look. And his parents thought *he* was messy!

"Molly's little friend Nadia has just started talking," Jenny went on. "We see her at Teeny-Time Song Group on Fridays. But she's three weeks older and not half as clever as Molly, is she, poppet?"

Bertie yawned loudly. "When's supper?" he asked.

His mum glared at him. "Bertie, can't you find something to do?"

"What?" said Bertie.

"Do some colouring or something."

"I don't have anything to colour. Can I watch telly?"

"Anyway," Jenny went on. "Simon and

Dirty Bertie

I have this little bet on what her first word will be. Simon thinks it will be 'Dad'. But I know it's going to be 'Mum', isn't it, Molly? Mum, mum, mum."

"It could be 'Poo'," said Bertie, unexpectedly.

"Pardon?" said Jenny, faintly.

"Poo," repeated Bertie. "I was just saying, her first word – it could be 'Poo'."

"Bertie!" said Mum.

"What? I'm only saying! Babies poo all the time."

Jenny covered Molly's ears with her hands.

"Bertie," she said. "Why don't you go next door and see what's on television?"

CHAPTER 3

Bertie spent the night in Molly's room.
Her cot had been moved next door into
her parents' room to make way for him.
Bertie slept on an air bed with a Bunny
night light on top of the drawers beside
him. Molly's room was painted baby pink
with a border showing the letters of the
alphabet. A mobile hung from the ceiling

with fluffy smiling sheep. Bertie got
out of bed. If you wound up the
mobile it played a tinkly version of
'Baa Baa Black Sheep' and the
fluffy sheep went round and
round, bobbing up and
down gently. He stood
on a chair to wind it
up to see if he could
make the sheep go
round faster. The door
of the room creaked
open.

"BEE
BEE!" cried
a voice
behind
him.

Dirty Bertie

Bertie was so startled he took a step
back and grabbed wildly at the mobile.
For a second, his foot hovered in the air,
then he fell back with the tangled sheep
on top of him.

"BUM!" he said loudly.

Molly bent over him. She was wearing
her pink bunny sleepsuit.

"BUM!" she said.

Bertie stared at her in horror.

Dirty Bertie

"What…?"

"Bum! Bum, bum, bum, bum…!" sang Molly, stamping her tiny feet. Bertie put a hand over her mouth to stop her.

"Shhh!" he whispered. "Naughty Molly. You mustn't say 'Bum'."

He took his hand away.

"Bum," repeated Molly, squashing Bertie's nose with her finger and giggling.

Bertie went to the door and pushed it shut. If anyone came in, he was in major trouble. He tried to think. Babies simply copied whatever you said, so surely he could teach Molly something else? He knelt in front of her and gave her a serious look.

"Molly," he said. "Say 'Bertie'. 'Bertie'. Say 'Bertie', Molly."

"Bum," said Molly.

"No! No bums, okay? Look, what's this, Molly? What's this?"

He waved the tangled ball of sheep in front of her. "'Sheep', Molly. 'Sheep'."

Molly grabbed the sheep and dropped them on the floor. "Bum!" she giggled.

Bertie stared at her. This was a nightmare. If Simon and Jenny found out their daughter's first word was "Bum",

they'd have a fit. They'd probably pass
out. Mum would go bananas – and he
was bound to get the blame. It would
be no use trying to explain it was an
accident. Parents never believed you.
He'd probably have his pocket money
cancelled for a month. Or a year. Maybe
for the rest of his life.

He looked around the room in
desperation and grabbed a toy puppy.

"Look, Molly, doggie! What does doggie say? Woof! Woof!"

He made the puppy tickle her under the chin.

"BEE BEE!" said Molly, grabbing the puppy and kissing it on the nose.

"Yes!" nodded Bertie. "That's right. Bee bee! Bee bee!" It was going to be okay. Babies never remembered things for long. They said a word and then a minute later they had forgotten it.

Molly was toddling over to the door. It was shut. She pointed at it, wanting to get out.

"BUM!"

CHAPTER 4

Bertie was exhausted. He'd spent the
entire morning playing with Molly. He'd
played with her toy farm. He'd played
Peepo behind the sofa. He'd watched
Fifi's Fairy Friends six million times. Jenny
said he was an angel. But the truth was
he didn't dare let Molly out of his sight
in case she said the unmentionable word.

Dirty Bertie

After lunch, Simon suggested they all take Molly to the children's playground at the park. Bertie was glad to get out of the house. He couldn't take much more of this. But if he could just manage to keep Molly busy for the afternoon, they could go home and he'd be off the hook.

Molly sat in one of the baby swings, but refused to let anyone except Bertie push her.

Mum, Dad, Simon and Jenny stood and watched.

A girl in a red coat ran over and sat on the swing next to Molly.

"Look, Molly, here's Nadia," said Jenny.

Nadia pointed to Molly. "Monny!" she said. "Monny!"

Nadia's mum beamed proudly. "Clever girl! There's your friend, Molly."

She pushed Nadia on the swing. "She's picking up so many words now," she told Jenny. "There's no stopping her. The other day she looked at me and said 'Biscuit', clear as you like."

"Amazing," said Jenny.

"I know, and every day it's something new. How about Molly? Talking yet?"

Jenny sighed. "Only baby words so far," she said. "But we don't want to rush her. This is her friend, Bertie, by the way. He's been a complete angel with Molly. Hasn't stopped playing with her all day."

Bertie hadn't been paying attention. Molly's swing had slowed down and almost stopped. She bounced up and down in her seat with frustration.

"BUM!" she cried.

"Pardon, sweetie?" said Jenny.

"Bum!" sang Molly. "Bum, bum, BUM!"

"Oh dear!" said Nadia's mum, trying not to laugh.

"Bum!" cried Molly.

"Bum!" shouted Nadia, joining in.

"No darling, we don't say that," said Nadia's mum. "We say 'Bottom'."

She turned to Jenny. "Really! I thought you said she wasn't speaking!"

"She wasn't," said Jenny, turning pink. "She's never said that before. I've no idea where she could have learned it."

"Nor me," said Simon.

Mum looked at Bertie grimly. "Oh, I think I can probably guess," she said.

Bertie decided it might be a good time to slip away.

"Um, will you excuse me?" he said politely. "I'm just going for a poo."

Dirty Bertie
BOGEYS!

For Lynsey ~ D R

For Olivia and Natasha –
with best Berties ~ A M

Contents

BOGEYS!

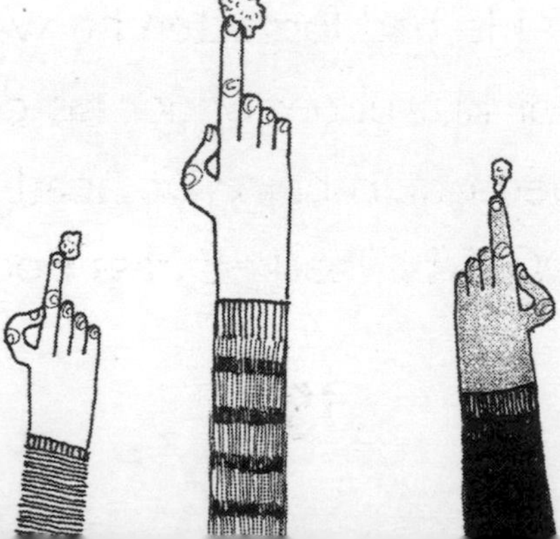

CHAPTER 1

"BERTIE!" Miss Boot thundered. "ARE YOU PAYING ATTENTION?"

Bertie shot upright.

CRACK!

"OW!" He had forgotten he was looking for his rubber under his desk. He peeped out, rubbing his head.

"SIT DOWN!" barked Miss Boot.

"Now what was I just saying?"

"When?" asked Bertie.

"While you were crawling around under your desk."

Bertie racked his brains trying to remember. The truth was he hadn't been following too closely. Whenever Miss Boot started talking, Bertie's mind had a habit of wandering off.

"Um, you were saying…" Bertie looked to Eugene for help. Eugene mouthed something he didn't quite catch.

"You were saying … about fried eggs."

The class sniggered. Eugene whispered in his ear.

"Oh, *Friday*. You were saying about Friday."

Miss Boot folded her arms. "Yes, and

what's happening on Friday? Do tell us."

Bertie hadn't the faintest clue. "We're having a day off," he said, hopefully.

More laughter.

THUMP! Miss Boot's fist slammed down on her desk.

"We are *not* having a day off. I was talking about our visitor. Can anyone tell Bertie who's coming to school on Friday?"

A sea of hands rose in the air. Miss Boot's eyes fell on the pale boy bouncing up and down in the front row like an eager puppy.

"Yes, Nicholas?"

"The Mayoress," said Know-All Nick.

"Quite right. I'm glad *someone* is paying attention," said Miss Boot.

Nick smirked at Bertie. Bertie scowled back.

Miss Boot went on. "It's a great honour to have someone as important as the Mayoress coming to our school. I'm sure you're all very excited."

Bertie yawned. Why were school visitors always so boring? Why didn't they invite someone interesting for a change – like a lion tamer or a brain surgeon?

"Now," said Miss Boot, eyeing the class,

Dirty Bertie

"Miss Skinner would like one of our class to do a special job. One lucky child is going to welcome the Mayoress in assembly. Who wants to volunteer?"

The hands shot up again. Bertie couldn't see what all the fuss was about. Know-All Nick was jiggling around as if he needed the toilet.

"Ooh, Miss, Miss! Me, me!" he gasped.

Dirty Bertie

Miss Boot hesitated. Last time there was a visitor she had chosen Nick to meet them. And the time before.

"Hands down," she said. "Since so many of you are keen, we will put all your names in a hat and draw one out."

Everyone wrote their name on a piece of paper and put it in a biscuit tin. (Miss Boot didn't actually have a hat.) Miss Boot drew out one scrap of paper and unfolded it. She read the name scrawled in big letters. She turned white. She looked as if she might pass out.

Dirty Bertie

"Who? Who is it?" everyone asked.

"Bertie," groaned Miss Boot.

Bertie looked up from doodling on his maths book.

"What? I wasn't doing anything," he said.

Miss Boot sighed. "If you were listening, Bertie, you'd know that you've been chosen to welcome the Mayoress."

"ME?" said Bertie. "*Really?*"

"Really," said Miss Boot. The bell went for break. She screwed up the piece of paper in her hand. She needed to find somewhere quiet to lie down.

CHAPTER 2

"*You?*" said Dad.

"*You?*" said Suzy. "They want *you* to meet the Mayor?"

"Actually, it's the Mayor-hess," Bertie said.

"But why *you?*" asked Suzy. "They had the whole school to choose from! Why didn't they pick someone with half a brain?"

Bertie ignored this remark. "Miss Boot thought I'd be good at it," he said. "Meeting mayor-hesses and that. Making speeches."

Dad looked horrified. "Surely they don't want you to make a speech?"

"I don't know yet," said Bertie. "We're having a practice on Thursday."

Mum put an arm round his shoulder. "Well, I think it's wonderful, Bertie," she said. "I'm very proud of you."

"Yes," said Bertie, sticking out his tongue at his sister. He hadn't mentioned that he had been selected by pure chance. It was a small detail.

Suzy still couldn't believe it. "Has your teacher got a screw loose?" she asked. "Does she *know* what you're like?"

"I don't see why you're making such a fuss," said Bertie. "All I've got to do is give her a bunch of old flowers. It's not difficult."

"Of course it's not," said Mum. "But it is the Mayoress and she is very important…"

"*I've* never heard of her," said Bertie.

"…And the whole school will be watching," Mum went on.

"Oh yes, I forgot," said Bertie. "Miss Boot says a man from the *Pudsley Post* is coming as well."

"The newspaper?"

"Yes, he's going to take my picture with the Mayor-hess."

Dirty Bertie

"Good heavens! Is that a good idea?" asked Dad.

Bertie frowned. He'd expected a bit more enthusiasm. He thought his family would be *pleased* that his picture was going to be in the paper.

"I'm sure it will all be fine," said Mum. "Just as long as you don't do anything … silly."

"Like what?" asked Bertie.

"Burping," said Suzy.

"Or talking with your mouth full," said Dad.

"And *please, please, please*, Bertie, don't pick your nose," pleaded Mum.

"I won't," said Bertie. "When do I pick my nose?"

"Only every five minutes," said Suzy, scornfully.

"Well, what does it matter? It's *my* nose," said Bertie. "It's not as if I go round picking any old nose!"

Mum rolled her eyes. "You just cannot do it. Not when you're meeting the Mayoress."

"I won't!"

"Or the other thing," said Suzy.

"What other thing?"

"You know – eating bogeys!" said Suzy. "It's disgusting!"

"I don't!"

"You do!"

Dad held up a hand. "In any case, nose picking is a horrible habit and it's time you gave it up," he said.

"I will," said Bertie. "But…"

"No buts," said Mum, firmly. "I want you to promise."

Bertie sighed heavily. "I promise," he said. "You won't catch me picking my nose again."

CHAPTER 3

Bertie went upstairs to his room,
humming to himself. He'd promised his
parents they wouldn't *catch* him picking
his nose – so he'd just have to make
sure he wasn't caught.

In any case, he didn't see what all the
fuss was about. Everyone picked their
nose. His friends certainly did. Bertie and

Dirty Bertie

Darren often compared bogeys to see who had the biggest. They'd invented several bogey games, including Bogey Golf, Bogey Table Football and Roller-Bogey.

Grown-ups picked their noses, too. Bertie had seen his dad do it when he was driving. And Miss Boot did it when she was reading a book. He bet even the Queen picked her nose when no one was looking.

Dirty Bertie

So what was the harm if Bertie sometimes had a good clean out? Talking of which, there was no one about now…

"BERTIE!" Mum stuck her head round the door. "Remember what you promised!"

"I wasn't!" cried Bertie. "I just had an itch."

Mum tutted. "I'm watching you."

Bertie flopped down on his bed. This was terrible. If you couldn't pick your nose in your own bedroom where could you do it?

Five minutes later, he slipped out of the back door. His Top Secret Hideout was behind the garden shed. Darren and Eugene were the only ones who knew about it and they were sworn to secrecy.

Dirty Bertie

Bertie pushed his way in among the
bushes and sat down. Alone at last.
Now for…

"BERTIE! What are you doing?"

Dad was staring at him through the
shed window.

"Nothing!" said Bertie. "I was just looking for Whiffer."

"He's asleep on the sofa. Come out of there! It's filthy!"

Bertie drooped back to the house. This was hopeless. His parents wouldn't leave him alone for five minutes. He was actually glad when it was time to go to bed.

Mum came up to tuck him in.

"Goodnight, Bertie!"

"Night, Mum."

"Sleep tight!"

CLICK! Off went the bedroom light. Peace and quiet at last. No one to disturb him. Bliss. Bertie's finger crept out from under the covers.

"BERTIE!" called Mum. "STOP PICKING YOUR NOSE!"

Dirty Bertie

CHAPTER 4

For the rest of the week, Bertie's parents watched him like vultures. He couldn't even lift a hand without Mum tutting or Dad glaring at him. He tried to find places where he could be by himself. On Tuesday Mum found him hiding in the towel cupboard. On Wednesday Dad caught him in Whiffer's kennel.

Dirty Bertie

School was just as bad. Miss Boot made him practise his part for assembly over and over again. She barked orders at him: "Don't slouch! Hands out of your pockets! Stop mumbling – SPEAK UP!"

Dirty Bertie

By the time Friday came round Bertie was beginning to wish he'd never been chosen. He wished he was sitting with his friends instead of standing at the front with a bunch of droopy flowers. He could see Darren and Eugene pulling faces at him. Darren put two fingers up his nose as a joke.

Dirty Bertie

The man from the *Pudsley Post* was
ready with his camera. Bertie shuffled
his feet nervously. What if he did
something wrong? What if he tripped
on the steps? Or trod on the flowers?
What if he forgot what to say?

The hall was hot and airless. Miss
Boot was frowning at him. More than
anything Bertie was *dying* to pick his
nose. He always picked his nose when
he was nervous and now it was like
having a terrible itch which you
couldn't scratch.

His nose felt bunged up. He was convinced he had a giant bogey poking out of one nostril. But he didn't dare investigate – not with the whole school watching.

A door opened and Miss Skinner entered, followed by the Mayoress.

Bertie had been expecting someone royal like the Queen. But the Mayoress could have been one of his gran's friends. She wore a plum-coloured dress, which matched her face. Round her neck was a large silver chain.

Dirty Bertie

She took a seat while Miss Skinner
turned to face the rows of children.

"We are extremely honoured – blah
blah blah," droned Miss Skinner.

Bertie had stopped listening. He'd just
noticed no one in the hall was looking
at him. They were all gazing up at the
Mayoress and her silver chain.

Go on, said a voice in Bertie's head.
One little pick. What harm can it do?
Bertie bent his head as if he needed to
scratch his nose. It didn't take more
than a few seconds.

"BERTIE!" hissed Miss Boot. "*Hurry up!
We're waiting!*"

Bertie dropped his hand. Had he
been spotted? He glanced round – no,
but Miss Skinner had stopped talking.
Everyone was waiting for him to

welcome the visitor. He thudded up the steps and on to the stage. He thrust the droopy flowers at the Mayoress.

"For-you-Miss-Mayor-hess-from-all-the-children," he gabbled in one breath.

"Oh! Thank you. How kind," smiled the Mayoress.

Bertie turned away. Everything might have been all right if he'd gone back to his place there and then. But he realized he'd forgotten something. He was meant to shake hands. He turned back and stuck out one sweaty hand. Bertie stared in horror. There was something stuck to the end of his finger: a giant green bogey.

The Mayoress had seen it, too. She bent closer to examine it.

"Oh! What is that?"

Dirty Bertie

"What?" asked Bertie.

"That *thing* stuck to your finger."

"Oh, er, that," said Bertie. "It's um …
it's a…"

And then he did it. The thing he
claimed he never did. The thing that no
one in the school who saw it happen
would ever forget. The thing you must
never do when someone is about to take
your picture for the paper…

CHAPTER 1

"Bagsy sit at the back!"

Bertie clattered up the steps on to the coach. It was the day of the school trip. Bertie loved going on trips. He loved the coach ride there, the packed lunches and pulling faces at passing cars. He loved drawing on the windows, stuffing crisps and fizzy drinks – and being sick on the way home. Best of all, a trip meant a whole day without boring lessons. No mouldy maths or dreary spelling! No hours of listening to Miss Boot droning on and on.

Today the class were going to Rustbottom Hall. Miss Boot said it was an Historic Building, hundreds of years old. Bertie couldn't wait. Last year, Darren's family had been to Cannonshot Castle. It had a moat and battlements and a headless ghost in the West Tower. There was even something called a joust, where real knights in armour fought each other on horseback. Bertie thought he'd make a brilliant knight. Sir Bertie of the Green Bogey. He would rescue princesses and slay fire-breathing dragons – Miss Boot had better watch out.

Bertie raced to the back
seat, only to find Know-All Nick and his
weedy pal, Trevor, had got there first.
They were sucking sherbet lemons.
Handing out sweets was the only way
Nick could get anyone to sit next to him.

"Too slow, Bertie," smirked Nick.

Bertie scowled and sat down next to Darren in the seats in front.

DOINK!

Something hit Bertie on the head and bounced off. He turned round.

"Did you throw that?"

"Throw what?" Nick gave him a sickly smile.

Bertie picked a yellow sweet off the floor. "This!"

"I don't know what you're talking about," sneered Nick. "Seen anyone throwing sweets, Trevor?"

"Er, no, Nick," said Trevor meekly.

"Liar," said Bertie.

"Frogface," replied Nick.

"Yeah, frogface," said Trevor.

"You wait…" said Bertie.

"BERTIE! I WON'T TELL YOU AGAIN! TURN ROUND!" thundered Miss Boot.

"But Miss, it wasn't me…"

"SIT DOWN! And if I see you turn round again, you will sit next to me."

Dirty Bertie

Bertie flopped back into his seat. He didn't want to sit next to Miss Boot. He'd rather sit in a bath of cold custard. All the same, he would get even with that sneaky know-all. Maybe Rustbottom Hall had a deep, dark dungeon? Maybe he could lock the door and leave Nick to the rats.

CHAPTER 2

The coach swung into the drive and came to a halt. Bertie trooped off with the rest of the class, eager to start exploring. He stared. Rustbottom Hall was a crumbly old house with a clock tower and a wonky weather vane. The roof was whitewashed with pigeon poo.

"*Is this it?*" asked Bertie.

Dirty Bertie

"Isn't it magnificent?" said Miss Boot. "This hall has been home to the Rustbottom family since the 17th century."

"But where's the moat?" asked Bertie.

"There isn't a moat."

"And where's the drawbridge?"

"It has a front door."

"But where are the knights going to do the jousting?"

Miss Boot gave Bertie a pained look. "Rustbottom Hall is not a castle," she snapped. "It is a house."

Dirty Bertie

A *house*? Bertie couldn't believe it. He'd been looking forward to seeing a real castle. Battling on the battlements. Rampaging round the ramparts. What was the point of coming all this way to see a crumbly old house? If he wanted to see a house he could have stayed at home!

"It's not like Cannonshot Castle," grumbled Darren.

"It's falling to bits," moaned Eugene.

"QUIET!" thundered Miss Boot. "Now, we will be having a short tour of the hall. After that we'll split into groups to do an exciting quiz. Follow me, class."

They trudged inside the hall. It was cold, dark and smelt of mothballs. There were podgy little angels painted on the ceiling.

Dirty Bertie

Dirty Bertie

"Remember," warned Miss Boot, "no running, no noise and you are not to touch anything. Everything in this house is old and very valuable."

Bertie plunged his hands into his pockets. This was the worst school trip ever. They'd had more fun last year at the sewage farm. At least Trevor had slipped and fallen in.

The tour of the house went on for ages. Twice the guide had to ask Bertie not to yawn so loudly. Afterwards, Miss Boot divided them into groups.

Bertie's group had Darren and Eugene (which was good), and Sandra (which was not so good).

"I don't want to be with Bertie,"

sulked Sandra. "I want to go with Lucy."

Miss Boot took no notice. She handed a worksheet to each group. It involved trailing around the hall to answer a list of questions. Bertie stared at it in horror. *Thirty* questions? It would take *days* to answer them all! He felt tired just looking at them.

"I don't have a pencil," he said.

"I told you to bring one," snapped Miss Boot.

Bertie searched his pockets. "I did. I must have lost it."

"Then share with Darren." Miss Boot glared at him. "Work as a group to answer the questions. And Bertie?"

"Yes, Miss?"

"Do *not* touch anything. Not even the door handles."

Dirty Bertie

Bertie trailed after
Darren, Eugene and
Sandra.

"Why can't I be the one
to write the answers?"
grumbled Sandra.

"It's my pencil,"
said Darren.

"Can't I borrow it?"

"No."

"Please?"

"No."

"You're mean and ugly
and I hate you," said Sandra.
"I want to be in Lucy's
group."

Bertie looked over
Darren's shoulder. "How
many have we done so far?"

Darren checked the sheet. "None."

Know-All Nick breezed past them. He
had brought his own pen and clipboard.
He was in a group with Trevor, Alice
and Mia.

"What's the matter? Stuck already,
Bertie?" jeered Nick in his reedy voice.

"No," said Bertie. "We've answered
loads."

"How many?"

"Three," lied
Bertie.

"We've done
four," boasted
Nick. "*And* we've
got them all right.
I bet we get loads
more right
than you."

Dirty Bertie

Bertie watched them hurry off in search of the next answer. He hated to be beaten at anything by Know-All Nick. He hadn't forgotten the time Nick had taken the part he wanted in the Christmas play. If Nick's team got top marks in the quiz, he would boast about it for weeks. Well, Bertie would show that smarty-pants show-off.

"We've got to beat them," he said. "We can't let them win."

"How?" asked Darren. "They've got all the brainboxes in their group."

"They haven't got me," said Bertie.

"Or me," said Eugene.

"Or me," said Sandra.

"No," said Darren. "Like I said, they've got all the brainboxes."

"How long have we got left?" asked Bertie.

Darren checked his watch. "Um … twenty … thirty … not that long."

"We'll have to speed up," said Bertie, taking charge. "If we whiz round we can find all the answers before them. Where to next?"

Darren checked the sheet. "The library."

CHAPTER 3

They charged along the corridor, with Bertie leading the way.

"How many books are there?" Darren read out.

Bertie looked at the shelves. "Millions."

"Better start counting then," said a sneering voice. Know-All Nick leaned in the doorway.

"We know the answer," he smirked.
"Want us to give you a clue?"

"No. Get lost." Bertie glared.

"It's *so* easy," said Know-All Nick.

"Yeah, easy-peasy," said Trevor.

"Come on," said Nick to his team.
"Let's leave the dunces to work it out."

Bertie's group charged upstairs. And
downstairs. Up more stairs. Along
corridors. Into broom cupboards. But
however fast they went, Nick's group
always got to the answer before them.

With time running out, they found
themselves on the top floor. Bertie
looked at their sheet. They'd left eight
questions blank and Darren had
doodled on two of them. Bertie didn't

feel that confident about the rest of
their answers either.

Q7: What was the name of the 5th Lord Rustbottom's wife?
A: Mrs Rustbottom

Q8: What are a pair of bellows used for?
A: Shouting

Q9: What is unusual about the guests' bathroom?
A: It smells of wee

Bertie sighed. There
was no way they were going to win. But
they couldn't just stand by and watch Nick
come top. They had to do something.

"Where are we?" said Eugene.

Bertie read a label on the wall. "The Blue Bedroom. And look, this is the last question: 'What can you see on the chamber pot?'"

"What's a chamber pot?" asked Darren.

Bertie pointed. "Look! By the bed!"

"Ha ha!" giggled Darren. "It's a potty!"

On a cabinet sat a pale-blue potty with a Chinese pattern.

"Dragons," said Bertie. "That's the answer. It's got dragons on it!"

"Brilliant!" Darren wrote it down in the box. "Do you think we're the first ones here?"

"Looks like it," said Eugene.

Suddenly Bertie had an idea. "Why don't we hide it?"

"What?" said Eugene.

"The potty. Then Nick's team will never get the answer."

Sandra stared. "Miss Boot said we weren't to touch anything."

"She'll never know," said Darren. "Anyway *we're* not going to touch it. Bertie will."

"*Me?*" said Bertie.

Darren shrugged. "It's your idea. And I'm doing all the writing, I can't do everything!"

"I'm not touching it," said Eugene, hastily.

"Nor me," said Sandra.

Bertie hesitated. If he got caught he'd be in major trouble. But it would be worth it to see Nick's face when he, Bertie, gave the right answer. He got down on his hands and knees to crawl under the rope barrier.

"Hurry up!" hissed Darren. "Before anyone comes."

"I am hurrying!" Bertie reached out and made a grab for the potty, knocking over a candlestick. It rolled across the cabinet and clattered on to the floor.

A moment later a much louder noise split the air.

DDDDRRRRRIIIIIINNNG!

Bertie turned pale.

"You've set off the alarm!" gasped Darren.

"Miss Boot'll kill you," said Eugene.

"Told you so," said Sandra.

Dirty Bertie

Bertie was dancing around with the potty in his hands. "What shall I do?" he cried.

"I don't know!" said Darren. "Hide it!"

Bertie looked around in desperation. He could hear voices approaching. Feet thundering up the stairs. Any moment now they would burst in and he'd be caught. He did the only thing he could think of. He unzipped his jacket and stuffed the potty inside.

CHAPTER 4

Miss Boot's gaze swept over the class like an icy wind.

"Some foolish person has set off the alarm," she said. "I trust *none of you* know anything about it."

The class shook their heads. Bertie tried not to look in Miss Boot's direction. He was sweating. Could she

see the big lump under his jacket? How
on earth was he going to smuggle the
potty back inside without getting caught?

"The staff are checking the house to
make sure nothing's missing," said Miss
Boot. "So, while we are waiting, let's go
through the answers to the quiz."

The class took out their sheets of
paper.

"Right," said Miss Boot. "Who can tell
me the answer to question one?"

Know-All Nick's hand shot into
the air.

Twenty minutes later, Nick's team had
scored 28 marks out of 29. Bertie's team
had scored two.

"Number 30, last question," boomed

Dirty Bertie

Miss Boot. "In the Blue Bedroom, what can you see on the chamber pot?"

Silence. Only one hand went up. It belonged to Bertie.

"Bertie?" said Miss Boot, surprised.
"You know the answer, do you?"

"Yes, Miss. It's dragons."

"Dragons?" Miss Boot checked her
sheet. "The answer I have is sea monsters."

Bertie was outraged. "No! Dragons."

"I'm sorry, I have sea monsters here."

"But they're dragons, Miss!"

"No arguing, Bertie."

"But Miss, they *are*!"

Miss Boot turned away. "Final scores then."

This was too much. Bertie unzipped his jacket.

"Dragons," he said. "Look, I'll show you!"

He held up the potty for everyone to see. Eugene covered his eyes.

Miss Boot's face turned white, then purple.

"BERTIE," she thundered. "WHERE DID YOU GET THAT?"

"Oh, um … I can explain," mumbled Bertie.

"Bring it here. NOW!" ordered Miss Boot.

Bertie pushed his way through the crowd. Now he was *really* for it. He was so busy worrying about his punishment, that he didn't see Know-All Nick stick out a leg.

Bertie tripped. The potty slipped from his grasp.

CRAAAASH!

There was a shocked silence. Bits of priceless potty littered the grass.

Bertie looked up at Miss Boot.

Dirty Bertie

"Whoops!" he said. "Good job it was only an old one!"

CHAPTER 1

"A present? For me?"

Bertie tore off the bag and stared at the black, shiny box.

☆ *The Marvo Magic Set* ☆

☆ *Amaze your friends!* ☆

"A magic set?" he gasped.

Gran smiled. "I saw it in a shop window and thought of you. Do you like it?"

Dirty Bertie

Like it? Bertie would have happily swapped his sister for a magic set. He'd always wanted to do magic. He ripped off the lid. Inside were cards, boxes and plastic cups – everything he needed to become a world famous magician. Bertie put on the black cloak and magician's hat. He waved his magic wand.

"Careful!" said Gran. "I don't want you turning me into a toad!"

Bertie stared at her. "You think I'll be able to do *real magic?*" he asked.

"Of course! With a bit of practice."

"Fantastic!" said Bertie.

The set came with the *Marvo Book of 101 Magic Tricks.* It was a fat book with a lot of pages. Bertie didn't have time to read it right now, he wanted to get started on some magic straight away.

Dirty Bertie

"Pick a card, Gran,"
he said, holding out
a pack. Gran took
a card.

"Don't let me
see it," said
Bertie. He screwed
up his eyes,
frowning hard.

"The King of
Hearts!" he said.

"Goodness!
So it is!" laughed
Gran.

"Really?" said Bertie, amazed.

"Definitely," said Gran. "The King of
Hearts. How on earth did you guess?"

"I don't know," said Bertie. "It must
be magic!"

Bertie could hardly believe it. *This is fantastic*, he thought. *All these years I had magic powers and I never even knew!*

He rushed into the kitchen.

"Mum! Mum! I can do magic!"

"That's nice," said Mum, sipping her coffee.

"No, listen — real magic! Ask me to make something disappear."

"OK ... what about this?" Mum held up a half-eaten chocolate biscuit.

"Watch!" said Bertie.

He closed his eyes and thought magic thoughts. He waved his wand three times. When he opened his eyes, the biscuit had vanished.

"See! I told you! Magic!" he said.

"That's amazing, Bertie!" said Mum, who seemed to have her mouth full.

Dirty Bertie

Bertie was on fire with excitement. He could do anything. He could turn his teachers to stone. He could make sweets grow on trees. He could make his sister his slave. Wait till he told his friends about this!

Dirty Bertie

Half an hour later, Bertie was standing in Eugene's garden.

"What are you going to do?" asked Eugene, nervously.

"Just a magic spell," said Bertie. "I've got to practise on someone."

"Why can't you practise on Darren?"

Darren shook his head. "It's best to start on someone smaller. Why don't you turn him into a spider?"

"No!" cried Eugene. "I don't like spiders!"

"A worm, that'll be easy, he looks like a worm," grinned Darren.

"All right," said Bertie. "Close your eyes."

"Promise it won't hurt?" said Eugene.

"Go on!"

Eugene reluctantly closed his eyes. Bertie covered his head with a black cloth.

"It's dark! I don't like it!" wailed Eugene.

"Keep your eyes closed! That's the magic cloth," said Bertie.

"It's not your hanky, is it? I don't want your germs!"

"Quiet!" said Bertie. "How can I do spells if you keep talking?"

Bertie frowned. He raised his magic wand and chanted the magic words:

Stinky pinky, ponky squirm,
Change Eugene into a worm!

He whipped off the magic cloth.

"ARGHH!" screamed Darren.

"What?" gasped Eugene.

"Just your ugly face!" hooted Darren. "Ha ha!"

Bertie couldn't understand it. He'd waved his wand and repeated the spell, so why hadn't it worked? When he'd tried the magic on Mum and Gran it had worked perfectly.

"You opened your eyes," he said.

"It's not my fault," said Eugene. "You must have said it wrong."

"This is boring. Let's do something else," yawned Darren.

"It will work," said Bertie. "I just need a bit more practice."

Just then, Eugene's mum stuck her head out of the back door.

"Bertie!" she called. "Your mum's on the phone!"

Bertie sighed. He pocketed his wand and went inside.

Darren watched him go.

"Hey, Eugene," he said. "Want to play a trick on Bertie?"

"What kind of trick?"

"A magic trick of course."

Eugene frowned. "Do I have to wear a hanky on my head?"

"You don't have to do anything," said Darren. "Listen, this is what we do…"

CHAPTER 2

Five minutes later, Bertie was back. He looked around in surprise.

"Where's Eugene?"

Darren didn't answer. His mouth was open in astonishment.

"L-l-look!" he said.

"What's the matter?"

"There! Look!"

Dirty Bertie

Bertie stared. Eugene's jumper lay on the grass. Something inside it was wriggling around. They both squatted down to take a closer look. A small pink head peeped out of the collar. It was followed by a long pink body.

"See?" gasped Darren. "It worked!"

"What?"

"You did it! You actually turned Eugene into a worm!"

Bertie stared. "*That's* Eugene?"

"It must be!"

"But he was here a minute ago!"

"I know. Then there was a flash of smoke and stuff – and the next minute he'd gone!"

Bertie stared at the tiny wriggling worm. "You're sure that's *him*?"

"Of course! That's his jumper, isn't it?"

"Wow!" said Bertie. "I did it! I actually did it! I told you I could do magic!"

The worm was wriggling its way across Eugene's jumper, trying to escape. Bertie picked it up, letting it wriggle on the palm of his hand. It was slimy and cold to the touch.

Bertie could see now that it was definitely Eugene. It had the same worried expression.

Dirty Bertie

"Careful," said Darren. "Don't drop him!"

Bertie cupped Eugene in both hands so he couldn't escape. This was incredible. Astonishing. He – the Amazing Bertie – had actually turned Eugene into a weeny wiggling worm. If he could do this, there was no limit to his magic powers. People would pay millions just to come and watch him perform…

"No hurry," said Darren, "but hadn't you better change him back?"

"What?"

"Change him back. You can't leave him like that. A blackbird might eat him."

Dirty Bertie

Bertie hadn't thought of that. Still, it shouldn't be that difficult for a master magician. If he could turn Eugene into a worm, changing him back would be a piece of cake. He set Eugene down and covered him with the magic cloth. He raised his wand and waved it three times in the air.

Biggly boggly, bogeys green,
Turn this worm into Eugene!

Bertie whipped off the magic cloth. The worm raised its head – or maybe its bottom, it was hard to tell. Bertie twiddled his wand.

"Um … maybe we just need to wait a few minutes," he said.

CHAPTER 3

The minutes ticked by. They were still staring at the worm on the grass.

"This is not good," said Darren. "This is a disaster. This is a—"

"Yes, OK, don't go on!" snapped Bertie.

He couldn't understand it. The spell had worked fine the first time, so what had gone wrong? Maybe he'd waved his wand too often or muddled the magic words. He tried the spell again – and again. Nothing happened. This was terrible. He'd changed Eugene into a wiggling worm and now he couldn't bring him back!

"What are we going to do?" he asked.

"Don't ask me," said Darren. "You're the magician!"

"It'll probably wear off," said Bertie, hopefully. "Spells don't last for ever, do they?"

"What if it doesn't?" said Darren. "What are you going to tell Eugene's mum? She'll go potty!"

"Shut up!" said Bertie. "I just need to think." He was pacing up and down the lawn. Maybe he should take Eugene home with him and consult his *Marvo Book of 101 Magic Tricks?*

Dirty Bertie

"EUGENE! Your supper's ready!"

Bertie froze in horror. Eugene's mum was coming down the path towards them.

"Quick – hide him!" hissed Darren.

Bertie scooped up Eugene and slipped him into his pocket.

Eugene's mum stopped and gave them a puzzled look.

"Where's Eugene? I thought he was with you?"

"No," said Bertie. "He … um … he went in to change."

"Change?"

"Yes, to change into something smaller," said Darren, grinning.

Bertie gave him a sharp kick. Eugene's mum was looking at them as if they were up to something.

"That's odd. I didn't see him come in," she said.

"Didn't you?" said Bertie. "Maybe he just sneaked past."

"Yes, probably *wormed* his way in," said Darren.

Bertie shot him a warning look. "Anyway," he said, "we've got to be going, haven't we, Darren?"

"Have we?"

"Yes. You know, my mum said I've got to go home…"

"URRGHHH!"

Eugene's mum had suddenly leaped backwards, as if she'd stepped in something nasty.

Bertie looked down and saw the worm dangling from his pocket. He was wriggling around, trying to escape. Bertie quickly pushed him back in.

Dirty Bertie

"There's a worm in your pocket!"
screeched Eugene's mum.

"Yes, he's my pet worm," said Bertie.
"He likes it in there."

"Bertie calls him Eugene, don't you,
Bertie?" said Darren.

"Um ... yes," said Bertie, turning red.
"Although he's not Eugene, obviously.
He's just a worm. Anyway, we better be
going..."

He backed away and fled up the
garden path.

CHAPTER 4

Back home, Bertie hurried to his
room and closed the door. He found
his old goldfish bowl – the one that
had belonged to his pet worm, Arthur,
before Mum threw him out – and filled
it with mud, leaves and a dollop of
peanut butter. Peanut butter was
Eugene's favourite.

Dirty Bertie

Bertie rushed downstairs. He found
the *Marvo Book of 101 Magic Tricks* in the
lounge and flicked through the pages.
There were card tricks, vanishing tricks,
mind-reading tricks … but not a single
mention of worms. Bertie threw the
book down in disgust. He was really
starting to worry now. What if Eugene
was stuck as a worm for ever? How was
he going to explain it to Eugene's mum?
She'd probably faint from the shock.

"BERTIE!"

Uh oh. Mum was calling.

"Bertie!" she yelled again. "Come here
this minute!"

Bertie trailed into the kitchen. "What?"

"Don't pretend you don't know. What
have I told you about keeping pets in
your room?"

Bertie turned pale. His mum was
holding a goldfish bowl – an empty
goldfish bowl.

"W-w-where is he?" he gasped.

"If you mean your revolting
worm, I threw it out in
the garden where
it belongs."

"Noooooooo!"
wailed Bertie.

Dashing outside, Bertie searched the
flower beds on all fours. Eugene might
be anywhere by now. He could have

crawled under a rock or been swallowed by a crow. And it would *all* be Bertie's fault. Eugene would never forgive him – especially if he was already dead. Bertie scrabbled around in the dirt. Out of the corner of his eye, he caught sight of something.

"Eugene!" Bertie had never been so relieved in his life. But wait a moment, there was more than one worm. There were three! Three fat pink worms – which was Eugene?

"Eugene?" said Bertie. "Speak to me! Wiggle your head if it's you!"

Dirty Bertie

The worms all wriggled, but not in a way that helped. It was no good. He would just have to keep all three until he could work out which one was Eugene. But where could he hide them? Not in his bedroom, Mum was bound to find them. It had to be somewhere she would never think to look. Bertie smiled to himself – he knew just the place.

DING DONG!

Bertie thumped downstairs and opened the door. Darren stood outside, grinning like mad.

"Hi, Bertie! Where's Eugene?" he asked.

"Shhh!" hissed Bertie. "Not so loud. He's safe upstairs."

"Really?" said Darren. "Are you sure?"

"Of course I'm sure," said Bertie.

"Are you sure you're sure?"

"What is this? What's so funny?" asked Bertie.

"SUR-PRISE!"

Suddenly somebody leaped out from behind the door.

It was Eugene! He looked pretty calm for someone who'd recently been wriggling around in a flower bed. Bertie stared at him in astonishment. "But … but…"

"Ha ha! Your face! Hee hee!"

Eugene and Darren were laughing so much they could hardly speak.

"But how?" stammered Bertie. "You're a worm! I hid you upstairs!"

Darren wiped his eyes.

"Don't be stupid," he said. "We played a trick on you."

"A trick?"

"It was Darren's idea," explained Eugene. "We found a worm and put it in my jumper. I was hiding in the bushes watching the whole time."

"And you believed it!" giggled Darren. "You *actually* believed it."

"I didn't really," said Bertie.

"You did!" hooted Darren. "You were in such a panic."

Bertie laughed. He had to admit it had been a clever trick.

"ARGGHHHHH!"

A deafening scream came from upstairs.

"What was that?" asked Eugene.

"That?" said Bertie. "That sounds like my sister. I think she might have found something in her drawer."

"BERTIE!" yelled Suzy.

"Come on," said Bertie. "I think it's time for a real magic trick. The one where I disappear!"

Look out for:

DAVID ROBERTS WRITTEN BY ALAN MACDONALD

Dirty Bertie PIRATE!